A&L Do Summer

A & L
do summer

JAN BLAZANIN

EGMONT
USA

New York

EGMONT
We bring stories to life

First published by Egmont USA, 2011
443 Park Avenue South, Suite 806
New York, NY 10016

Copyright © Jan Blazanin, 2011
All rights reserved

1 3 5 7 9 8 6 4 2

www.egmontusa.com
www.janblazanin.com

Library of Congress Cataloging-in-Publication Data

Blazanin, Jan.
A & L do summer / Jan Blazanin.
p. cm.
Summary: In Iowa farm country, sixteen-year-old Aspen and her friend
Laurel plan to get noticed the summer before their senior year and are
unwittingly aided by pig triplets, a skunk, a chicken, bullies, a rookie
policeman, and potential boyfriends.
ISBN 978-1-60684-191-4 (pbk.) — ISBN 978-1-60684-243-0 (e-book)
[1. Friendship—Fiction. 2. Conduct of life—Fiction. 3. Bullies—Fiction.
4. Family life—Iowa—Fiction. 5. Domestic animals—Fiction. 6. Iowa—
Fiction.] I. Title. II. Title: A and L do summer.
PZ7.B61636Aac 2011
[Fic]—dc22
2010043616

Printed in the United States of America

CPSIA tracking label information:
Printed in March 2011 at Berryville Graphics, Berryville, Virginia

To my favorite brother Dan

A&L Do Summer

one

"JUST IMAGINE IT, ASPEN." LAUREL WALKS BESIDE ME WAVING her arms. I feel like a football player, dodging her flapping hands and the lunatics rushing to their lockers. "It's Monday morning. Principal Hammond arrives at dawn with his briefcase in one hand and his thermos of coffee in the other—"

"I'm pretty sure Principal Hammond doesn't drink coffee." I clutch my notebook tighter against my chest to protect my advanced chemistry take-home final. After sweating bullets over it for three precious hours last night, I'm not about to risk losing it. "Once when I was picking up copies from the office, I overheard the secretary kidding him about being addicted to Mountain Dew."

Laurel gives me her freakish one-eye roll, and my neck hairs stand in frightened little rows. Something has to be wrong with a person who can roll her left eye sideways while the right one is staring straight ahead.

I smack her on the back of the head, not hard, just enough to make her focus both eyes on me. "Don't do that! You know it creeps me out!"

"Thanks for being so sensitive about my wandering eye, Skeleton Girl." Laurel punctuates her insult with an elbow between my ribs.

I elbow her back. "You're just jealous because I can still wear my training bra from sixth grade, and you outgrew yours."

She laughs and tosses her layered, strawberry-colored hair. Her normal color is a perfectly acceptable auburn, but Laurel shies away from anything resembling normal. "Okay, you got me there. Now stop interrupting while I'm running through my plan. Once you hear it, you'll be speechless. It's brilliant."

Now it's my turn to roll my eyes—both eyes at once like an ordinary person. Laurel and I have been friends since she and her dad moved into our development at the end of last summer. The first time I saw her toothy smile and spiky yellow hair—last summer's color—I was sure she'd add some much-needed sparkle to my basically drab life. And I was right, although sometimes Laurel's sparkle is more like a blinding glare.

Switching gears from Chicago to Cottonwood Creek, Iowa, hasn't been easy for Laurel. I've tried to give her the benefit of my experience as a lifetime resident, but she likes to make her own way and her own mistakes. Which is fine, as long as her mistakes don't include me.

We stop at our lockers in the section designated for juniors, and Laurel raises her voice to be heard over the din. "As I was saying, Principal Hammond enters the building at dawn. He walks down the darkened hallways to his office and inserts his key into the lock—"

"The custodians come in at five thirty and turn the lights on. So it's not dark when—" The green fire shooting from Laurel's eyes cuts off the rest of my explanation.

"He inserts his key into the lock," she repeats, "opens the door, and screams in terror as a flock of pigs comes squealing out!"

"Pigs? How do pigs get into Mr. Hammond's office?" Which is the world's stupidest question because I already know what Laurel is going to say.

Laurel lowers her voice to a loud stage whisper. "We wait until the night custodian goes off duty at eleven, sneak into the school with three or four pigs, and herd them right into Hammond's office." She hooks her fingers into the belt loops of her ultra-tight jean shorts. "Is that the best prank ever or what?"

"Laurel, that is hands down the stupidest idea you've ever had!" I say it louder than I intend to, but nobody notices. The sad truth is that none of them would notice if I did a handstand in the middle of the hall. Okay, a few folks might give that a glance, but then they'd yawn and keep walking.

Laurel's jaw drops. "How can you say that? It's a brilliant plan. If hiding a flock of pigs in the principal's office doesn't get us noticed, nothing will." Her eyes narrow suspiciously. "Or are you jealous because you didn't think of it?"

"Give me a break, Laurel. That isn't a plan. It's a sort-of-maybe idea."

The corners of her mouth pull down, and I take pity on her. "I admit that hiding pigs in Principal Hammond's office would be hilarious, but you're ignoring a few logistical details."

"Such as?" she demands.

"Such as, where do we find the herd of pigs—birds flock, pigs don't—and, once we do, how do we haul them into town? It's not like there's a pig farm on the next block, you know." I slide my notebook in front of my midsection in case Laurel decides to slug me. "And even if we solved those two problems, how do we break in without setting off the alarm?"

"That's an easy one," says a nasal voice from behind me. "When the alarm sensors zero in on your ugly-ass face, they'll explode into a million pieces."

Looking over my shoulder, I see the source of this witticism—Ferret Baumgarten, a senior with bug eyes and a pointed snout, whose IQ registers entirely to the right of the decimal point. He and my brother, Manny, have been classmates and sworn enemies since junior high. And today it looks like I'm the lucky recipient of one of Ferret's random acts of loathsomeness.

I do a quick scan of the hallway to make sure Ferret's buddies Buster and Kong aren't with him. By himself, Ferret is nothing but a loud mouth attached to a wimpy body. Kong's the size of a semi, but it's hard to be scared of someone so stupid he needs a GPS to find the guys' bathroom. But when Buster orders the two of them around, bad things happen. He has dead eyes and a tight-lipped sneer, and he only smiles when he's hurting someone. I don't like to think about what makes him laugh.

Laurel puffs up like a kitten on the attack. "Nobody was talking to you, Ferret. As usual. Go slink into your ferret hole and chew on some crickets or whatever it is rodents eat."

Sweat beads on Ferret's unibrow. Overactive sweat glands are one of his more attractive features. "My name is Mitchell," he hisses. "Mr. Baumgarten to you, Oak Scab. Or are you Maple Fungus?"

"That so-called joke is so stale it's fossilized," I say, not much louder than a whisper.

5

Laurel grins at me. "Nice one."

The brown hairs sticking out of Ferret's nose twitch like whiskers. "And the only people pulling end-of-the-year pranks will be graduating seniors."

"That's too bad." Laurel's voice drips honey. "Then you'll be home all alone while the rest of the seniors are out pranking."

Ferret's buggy eyes track toward the ceiling as he tries to process the insult. I can tell when he figures it out because his breath bursts out in a slobbery hiss. "You . . . You . . . stay out of my way, both of you, or—"

"We'll be sorry?" Laurel finishes for him. "Too late for that. I've been sorry since the first time I saw you."

With a tooth-baring snarl, Ferret skitters away, muttering angrily to himself.

"There goes your last best opportunity for a summer romance, Laurel," I say as we watch him go.

Laurel grabs her French book and slams her locker shut. "What can I say, Aspen? In a war of wits, poor old Ferret is seriously low on ammunition."

two

THE REST OF THE DAY PASSES PRETTY MUCH LIKE YOU'D expect for the third-to-last Friday of the school year. Everyone is impatient for summer, and my mood swings between elation and depression. For me, elation is handing in my advanced chem final, which signals the end of suffering in that class. Depression is knowing I have to endure three finals next week. On the plus side, we don't have snow days to make up, which means school gets out the Thursday before Memorial Day.

After school I keep Laurel company while she waits to talk to Ms. Harcastle, the American lit teacher, about a paper she claims Ms. Harcastle lost. Knowing Laurel, the paper probably didn't get written, but that won't stop her from arguing the point to her grave. Somebody's mother has Ms. Harcastle's ear, so we're hanging out in the hall until they finish talking.

The building is deserted except for the custodians and a few stragglers like us. Laurel's practicing what she's going to say to Ms. Harcastle, and I'm gazing at the wall and picturing two months of freedom, relaxation, and wild make-out sessions with an as-yet-unknown hunky guy who worships me.

My daydreams are capsized by a chugging noise, sort of like the world's smallest tugboat towing an ocean liner. I look around and see Mrs. Noonbottom, the vocal music teacher, steaming toward me. Mrs. Noonbottom is a Cottonwood Creek institution. Nobody knows how old she is, but she taught my parents in middle school. Nana Rosie swears Mrs. Noonbottom directed the choir at her high school graduation fifty years ago, but I'm almost positive she's making that up.

Not only is Mrs. Noonbottom as ancient as the *Titanic*, but her rear is the same size. As usual, she's wearing an out-of-style flowered dress that probably fit her a decade ago. It cuts into all the wrong places, and it's about a foot too short. So when she bends over . . . Well, if you can't guess her nickname, you don't deserve to know.

I took choir my freshman and sophomore years, until I realized the only two cute guys in the class were a couple.

So I dumped choir for advanced chem, where guys are plentiful and girls are few. By the time I discovered that their superior numbers didn't work to my advantage, it was too late to switch back.

Just as my choir experience ended, Laurel's began. She's too bubbly to be a serious-minded choir person, but she wasn't here for last spring's tryouts for Sound Wave, which is Cottonwood Creek's varsity show choir. Sound Wave's director, Mr. McNear, choreographs super-hot singing and dancing routines, and the members get lots of time out of class to perform in other schools. Last month Laurel tried out for next year's Sound Wave and nailed it. She wanted me to try out too, but since I dance like Kermit the Frog I took a pass.

I hope Mrs. Noonbottom will chug on by. Instead she stops and peers at us through her thick bifocals. "Good afternoon, girls." The *s* whistles through her dentures. "If you're here for freshman orientation, I'm afraid it was last week."

"Mrs. Noonbottom, I'm Aspen Parks. I sang in your choir last year—and the year before that."

"Really." She slides her glasses to the tip of her nose. "You've certainly changed."

I wish. Except for clean socks and underwear, I haven't changed since eighth grade.

"And I'm Laurel Piedmont." When Laurel sees Mrs.

Noonbottom's confused expression, she adds, "I sang a solo at last month's concert."

"Yes, of course. You have a lovely voice," Mrs. Noonbottom says absently. "It was lovely chatting with you girls. Now I must go home and feed my lovely parakeets, Mozart and Chopin." With a wiggle of her fingers she motors on.

"Did you hear that?" Laurel demands as soon as Mrs. Noonbottom is out of earshot. "'Freshman orientation was last week, you lovely, lovely girls.'" Her imitation of Mrs. Noonbottom is perfect, right down to the whistling dentures. "I was in her class less than an hour ago, and she doesn't even recognize me!"

"Who cares?" Although I'm more rattled than I'll admit that a teacher I had for two classes doesn't recall my existence. "She's a thousand years old. I'd be surprised if she recognized Mr. Noonbottom."

"That's not the point." Laurel frowns. "I've done everything possible to get noticed in this school. I wear cute clothes, I'm friendly, I don't smell bad." She sniffs her armpit to be sure. "Even before Dad and I moved here last summer I sent Facebook friend requests to every person in the Cottonwood Creek High network. And all of them accepted."

"So that's why you're Facebook buddies with Buster and Ferret." Another of life's mysteries solved.

10

Laurel tugs on one of her silver hoop earrings so hard I wince. "Also not the point, but yeah."

"Now that you know what jerks they are, why don't you—"

"It's for our own protection. If I unfriend them, I won't know what twisted stuff they're into." Laurel lets go of the earring and crosses her arms over her chest. "As I was saying before you interrupted, I've been knocking myself out all year to become popular, but I'm still a nobody."

I've lived here forever. What does that say about me?

"Not true," I say. "This morning Ferret made a special effort to tell you hello."

The parent who was talking to Ms. Harcastle stalks out and slams the door, which doesn't bode well for Laurel.

"I'm not joking," Laurel says with her hand on the doorknob. "We're going to make our mark on Cottonwood Creek this summer, no matter what it takes."

Despite my romantic daydreams, this is going to be like every other dateless, boring weekend of my high school career. Which is what you'd expect for a girl with limp brown hair and a chest like an ironing board. While guys might not mind me as a lab partner, anything beyond that is out of the question. On the plus side, not dating gives me time for important things like doing homework, cleaning my room, and bleaching the hair on my arms. Other girls drag into class Monday morning worn out from partying all weekend, but I have the satisfaction of knowing my room is clean and my arm hair is pale and silky.

I quickly discover that my boring weekend won't be relaxing, either. Mom is crazed about Manny's graduation and open house next weekend. She rousts Manny and me out of bed on Saturday morning at the ungodly hour of seven to "spiff the place up," as she puts it. By the time we shuffle downstairs, Dad is outdoors on a ladder, painting the trim on the windows.

"Jeez, Mom, why did you get us up in the middle of the night? Graduation isn't for another week," Manny grumbles as he steps over Carmine, our hairy brown-and-white dog, who is crashed in front of the refrigerator door, as usual. Manny slides Carmine out of the way with his foot and pulls out a carton of grapefruit juice. He's wearing baggy athletic shorts and a threadbare T-shirt, and I'm disgusted to see that he already has a golden tan and blond highlights from working at the golf course. The sun turns my hair to straw and my skin watermelon red. "If we clean today, we'll have to do it over again next weekend."

As a matter of principle, I try not to agree with Manny, but this time he's right. "Yeah, Mom. Why don't we wait until next Friday?"

Mom looks up from scrubbing the stovetop. Her grayish brown hair is squashed flat from the ugly hat she wears on her morning walk. Sweat is trailing down her cheeks, and there's a smudge of grease under her nose. "I'm the luckiest woman in the world. Look at my considerate children volunteering to pitch in on the chores! As long as it's not today."

The way I look at it, parents should be banned from using sarcasm because of the psychological damage it does to their children. I'm one of the lucky few who turned out okay, but I doubt that Manny will ever be normal.

Manny throws up his hands. "Fine, Mom, but I can only help you until eleven because I have to be at work by noon." He dumps half a box of strawberry-flavored cereal into a bowl. The sound of crinkling paper rouses Carmine, who groans to his feet, shakes loose hair and fleas all over the kitchen, and lumbers to the table to beg. "And I'm tied up all day tomorrow, mowing greens in the morning and caddying until dark."

He tosses a few cereal clusters to Carmine and empties a carton of milk into the bowl, except for the pint or so that splashes onto the floor. "So even though this morning is my only free time all weekend and I have to change the oil in my car, flush the cooling system, and rotate the tires, I'll help you instead." He shoves a spoonful of cereal into his mouth and proceeds to talk around it. "The oil light has only been flashing since Tuesday, so it's probably good for another week or so until the engine blows up."

Mom stops in mid-scrub. "It certainly is not! As soon as you finish eating, you will march right out there and take care of your car. And before you drive anywhere, your father is going to double-check that it's in proper working order."

When Mom goes back to scouring, Manny breaks into a grin. He treats that old black car of his better than he treats Cynthia, his girlfriend. I'm positive no lights were flashing when he gave Laurel and me a ride home from school Thursday. But if I mention it, that's my last ride of the summer. Mom and Dad are stingy with their car keys, and I can't afford my own car, so I have to stay on what passes for Manny's good side.

"What about you, Aspen?" Mom throws over her shoulder. "Any reason you can't pull weeds and trim the bushes?"

Before answering, I take a moment to show Manny the new pink polish on my right middle finger. "None that I can think of."

"Good. Then hurry up and eat so you can get started."

Except for food and water breaks—and monitored trips to the bathroom—Mom has Dad and me laboring like indentured servants all day Saturday and Sunday. Late Saturday afternoon it occurs to me that I might get out of Sunday's chores by reminding Mom I have three finals next week.

My excuse almost works until she checks the Cottonwood Creek High Web site and discovers my first final isn't until Wednesday. I should have known showing her how to access the site would come back to haunt me.

My back throbs from pulling weeds in the flowerbeds and spreading at least fifty bags of mulch. My neck and shoulders ache from steadying the electric hedge trimmers. My shins are bruised from leaning against the ladder when I washed the upstairs windows. And those jobs pale in comparison to scrubbing the grout between the tiles in the guest bathroom. I hope I got all the cleanser rinsed out of the toothbrush I used, or Manny's going to be really pissed.

The worst part of putting in all this work for Manny's graduation party is that he'll be away at college next year when mine rolls around. So guess who gets to do all the manual labor again?

Mom doesn't unshackle me until almost dark on Sunday. By then I barely have the strength to shower, change into my sleep tee, and crawl into bed. Carmine, who's exhausted from being under my feet every second for the past two days, is snoring on the rug. It's a good thing I have Laurel's number on speed dial because my fingers are too sore to push more than one button.

Laurel answers on the first ring. "It's about time you called! I've left you, like, a hundred messages. I thought you were coming over this afternoon." Her guilt-inducing moan works great on her dad, but it's wasted on me.

Laurel's parents divorced when she was nine. They had joint custody, but she mostly lived with her mother until her mom married a widowed guy with twin eleven-year-old boys. After a few months of coping with her prepubescent stepbrothers, Laurel was losing it. So when her dad moved here to be branch manager of the First Bank of Iowa, Laurel held her nose and jumped in. Cottonwood Creek lacks the excitement of Chicago, but her dad is way more easygoing than my parents. And he hires people to clean and mow the lawn. Compared to me, she has it easy.

I slide an extra pillow under my head. "Sorry. Mom had Dad and me working our butts off all weekend getting ready for Manny's graduation party. This is the first chance I've had to call you."

"Your parents are really into the whole child labor thing. Did you at least earn enough to buy a new outfit?"

"Almost." Laurel gets $50 a week from her dad for simply existing. I'm too embarrassed to admit that Mom and Dad don't believe in paying for chores. "But I'll make more when I work at the Sub Stop this summer."

"Maybe I'll get a summer job, too. If I don't, I'll drop dead of boredom."

"I'm just glad you're not spending the summer with

your mom in Chicago." My spirits perk up. At least I won't have to endure another deadly boring Cottonwood Creek summer by myself.

"Ten weeks with the twin terrors? God, no!" There's a pause so long I wonder if Laurel has fainted from horror. "Sorry, I had to plug my iPod into the charger," she says. "This is my first summer in Cottonwood Creek and our last summer in high school. We're going to soar from the depths of anonymity to the peak of notoriety. By September, Aspen Parks and Laurel Piedmont will own this town."

I'm too tired to think of soaring anywhere. "But stashing pigs in the school building is out, right? Because aside from the complications I mentioned, that stunt would put us on the fast track to expulsion."

"Definitely out. Not classy enough for us."

Laurel actually took my advice!

"We need something with more flash," she continues, "like painting our names across the water tower in the school colors. You can be navy and I'll be gold. See, I was thinking—"

"Good-bye, Laurel. See you at school tomorrow."

I snap my phone shut and lie back on my pillows. Where does Laurel get her ideas?

three

THE BABY DRAGON I FOUND ON THE PATH IS CUPPED IN MY *palm. Her blue-green scales feel cool and moist, but flames shoot from her ruby eyes. Her heart vibrates with terror, and nothing I say calms her. Faster and faster her heart quivers until I fear it's going to fly from her chest. "Shush," I whisper. "It's okay. Sh—"*

Two strong arms hold me down and a long, wet tongue slides into my open mouth. My assailant's breath smells of rotted meat; his jaw is rough with stubble. Choking and sputtering, I push him away. But there's no escape. He pins me down and slurps my neck.

"Carmine! What the—!" I roll onto my side and shield my face with my arms. Undaunted, Carmine sticks his nose into my ear and squirts it full of dog snot.

"Stop it!" I vault out of bed, rubbing my slimy ear. My alarm clock shows 12:17. "It's the middle of the freaking night!"

But Carmine has moved on to other interests. Now he's nosing something beside my pillow. So help me, if he dragged another mangled chipmunk through the dog door . . .

I edge away from the bed in case I need to run for it. The whatever-it-is gleams with reflected moonlight, which is a good sign. Dead animals are rarely reflective.

The object vibrates, and Carmine whines. I snatch it up and check the caller ID. My heart is still racing from being jolted from sleep by French kisses laced with dog food. "It's after midnight! Is everything okay?"

"If you want to be expelled from school, everything's fabulous." Laurel's voice is muffled, as if she's cupping her hand around the phone. "Otherwise, we're in deep trouble."

Laurel's hysterics are legendary. Unless weekend toilet scrubbing has become a reason for expulsion, I've got nothing to worry about. I stifle a yawn and climb back into bed. "Why are you whispering?"

"Because I don't want the neighbors to hear me," she hisses.

"What are you doing, camping out in your backyard?"

"No. I'm standing in your front yard. Now get your butt down here or our lives will be completely ruined."

She hangs up.

Something tells me that the chances of having my life ruined are a lot smaller if I stay in bed. But Laurel will just keep calling—or throwing rocks at my window—until I go downstairs and hear her out. I put on a pair of shorts and my flip-flops. Then I change my mind and decide to carry the shoes until I get outside.

I point my index finger at Carmine's nose and use my sternest voice. "Stay, Carmine." Which is just as effective as telling pigeons not to poop on statues. He races past me and is waiting at the bottom of the stairs. By blocking him with my foot, I manage to trap him inside the house as I edge out the door.

Laurel is pacing back and forth on our front walk. As soon as she sees me, she rushes over and clamps onto my arms. "They're going to do it! I saw them! And we'll get blamed for the whole mess."

Her eyes are spinning like whirligigs. "Okay, Laurel, you need to slow down," I say in a soothing voice. "Take three deep breaths and tell me what happened, from the beginning."

She drops my arms. "Why are you talking like that? You sound like a zombie on downers."

So much for my career in psychology. "Forget it. Just tell me what's so urgent." It's damp and chilly, and hungry mosquitoes are circling.

"That's what I was trying to do before you went all

undead on me," Laurel says in a huff. "See, I was taking the trash can out to the curb about ten minutes ago. I was supposed to do it after lunch, but I forgot until I was almost asleep. So I thought I'd sneak out and take care of it because I won't have time in the morning. And Dad's been hinting that he's going to buy me a car, so I didn't want to get on his bad side, you know. That's when I saw them! Right away I heard the squealing, and I knew they were going to do it."

I feel like I'm riding upside down on a roller coaster. "Them who? What squealing? Going to do what?"

"Put the pigs in Principal Hammond's office, of course!" Laurel stamps her foot in exasperation. "Buttferk— you know, Buster, Ferret, and Kong—drove by in Buster's dumpy white pickup truck. I couldn't actually see the pigs because I guess they're too short. But I heard that loud squealing, and I know they're going to do it and we'll be blamed!"

That's it? "Relax, Laurel. So Ferret overheard us talking about a prank involving pigs. It's not our fault if he decides to act on it. Besides, he's the only person who knows what we said, so it's his word against ours. And nobody's going to . . ."

Laurel's looking everywhere but at me, and her face has gone whiter than the moon.

A grapefruit-size lump drops into my stomach. "Ferret is the only person who knows, isn't he?"

She runs her sweatshirt zipper up and down. "Sure.

Except for maybe a few people who might have read my post in their news feed."

My eyes jump out of their sockets. "You posted your pig idea on Facebook?"

"Kind of. But I didn't get that many comments from the kids around here." Still not looking at me, she yanks the cords in her hood back and forth.

"You posted it once?" She nods. "And that's the only place, right?" The lump in my stomach is doing jumping jacks. "Right, Laurel?"

"It was such a good idea, you know, that I wanted everyone to know I thought of it. That was, like, before you pointed out all the things that could go wrong. . . ."

"Let me guess—you sent a fan request to all four hundred ninety-three of your friends." This is what happens when I spend my time studying and doing chores instead of keeping track of my news feed.

"Facebook calls it a 'Like' instead of a fan request now, remember?" She swallows. "And I might have Tweeted about it two or three times—"

I clap my hand over Laurel's mouth to keep from strangling her. "Stop! I don't want to hear any more."

Laurel pries my fingers off her face. "You might as well know the rest. About half an hour ago I got a Facebook message from Ferret from his phone. See, he has to go through Facebook because my phone number is private. And you say

I can't keep a secret," she adds with a smug little grin.

I cross my arms and give her the death stare.

Her smile falters. "Anyway, he said Buster liked my idea so much that Buttferk is going to do it. You know, put pigs in Principal Hammond's office. So I messaged back that they needed to drop the idea because I'd tell everyone they did it instead of us."

"And?"

"Ferret said it would be too bad if somebody broke into our garage and slashed my dad's tires." Laurel's eyes shine with tears. "He said if somebody got pissed enough, they might not stop with the tires."

My mouth goes dry. "Why didn't you tell me that five minutes ago?"

"I thought if I kind of led up to it, you wouldn't be as mad," she says between sniffs.

I don't have time to argue with Laurel's twisted logic. "And you're sure it was Buster's truck?"

"Positive. It had that big circle of rust on the driver's-side door." Laurel wipes her eyes on her sweatshirt sleeve.

Adrenaline sends me into overdrive. "Is your bike here?" She points to where it's parked in our driveway. "I'll get mine out of the garage."

She runs to keep up as I hurry to the garage and roll my bike out the side door. "What are we going to do?"

"I have no idea." As I swing my leg over my bike, a

breeze reminds me that I'm wearing nothing except my thin sleep tee and gym shorts. "Hold on. I'm not wearing a bra."

Laurel stares pointedly at my pointless chest.

"Yeah, you're right. Nothing to worry about here."

four

EVEN THOUGH GOING BRALESS MIGHT NOT BE AN ISSUE, a jacket would have been a good idea. The cool wind billows under my tee, peppering my chest and stomach with goose bumps. Pretty soon my teeth are chattering, but that could be caused by blind fear instead of cold.

The town seems deserted except for a yellow cat that crouches on the curb and watches as we ride past. Cottonwood Creek isn't what you'd call bustling, but it's eerie not to see any traffic at all. Laurel and I race in and out of the shadows of maple, oak, and cottonwood trees twice as high as the streetlights. We pass my favorite house—a massive two-story that was the mayor's mansion a hundred years ago. When I was a kid it reminded me of a dollhouse with its fancy shutters and steep red roof. It's set back from the street on a long, winding driveway, and I can barely make it out in the dark.

The streets around the town square are paved with red brick from the Turner Brick and Tile Factory west of town. Cottonwood Creek's historic brick streets are one of its few claims to fame. They're cool to look at, but riding a bike on them is murder. Besides causing butt bruises, some of the cracks are wide enough to trap a bike tire and flip you over. That happened to me when I was eleven, and I have a scar on my left knee to prove it.

My butt isn't my only unhappy body part. My thighs are burning, and my shoulder muscles are sending out angry messages. I pull in a deep breath and catch the sickly sweet odor of a catalpa tree. The pavement is white with fallen blossoms that squash and stick to my tires. As we pass under it, Laurel tilts back her head and sniffles. It's so late all the birds are asleep except for a mourning dove, wondering who is idiotic enough to be up and out at this time of night. I wish I didn't know the answer.

We're two blocks from the high school when an eerie, rolling howl soars over the treetops. Laurel gasps. "What's that awful sound?"

"That awful sound is Carmine tracking us. I forgot to block the dog door." So much for the element of surprise.

"What happened to the fence around your backyard?"

"That's just for show. If Carmine wants out, he goes over the top."

"Well, at least we have him for protection if something goes wrong." Which is optimistic even for Laurel.

If killer chipmunks ambush us, we're safe as can be. Anything bigger, and we're on our own.

An engine guns nearby, and I hear a squeal that has nothing to do with pigs. "Laurel, somebody's coming. Get off the street!"

I make a sharp turn into the nearest yard and smash through a thin spot in the hedge. Dozens of sharp little twigs rake my skin and snag my clothes. A few feet away, Laurel crashes into a thicker section of the hedge and bounces through a shower of leaves and spiderwebs. We hit the ground commando-style as a rusty white pickup screeches into sight. Laurel pokes her head up for a better view while I peer through the hedge.

As the pickup passes under the streetlight, the driver spits a stream of tobacco juice, leaving a slimy brown trail down his door. I recognize the flabby face as belonging to Buster Reese, who, in addition to his charming personality, has the distinction of being Cottonwood Creek's oldest senior. Rumor is that he flunked all his classes again this semester, but teachers threatened to strike if they has to deal with him another year. So Principal Hammond has to let him graduate.

Laurel makes a retching sound. "Could he be any more disgusting?"

"Not without cloning himself," I say, brushing twigs from my sleep tee and shorts. "Did you see if anyone else was with him?"

Laurel pulls a handful of leaves from her hair. "I caught a flash of Ferret's pointy face in the back of the truck just before a giant arm jerked him down. I'm going to take a wild guess the arm belonged to Kong."

"If Ferret and Kong are in the truck bed, then the pigs . . ."

As I reach down to pick up my bike, Carmine bounds through the hedge, plants his front paws on my shoulders, and covers my face and neck with rank-smelling slobber. "Stop it, Carmine! Get down!" I whisper-shout while trying to push him off. It takes a few minutes to get him calm enough to let me climb on my bike.

Cottonwood Creek High is centered on a spacious, tree-filled lot near the west end of town. Unfortunately, decades of trampling feet have decimated all but the hardiest weeds on what was once probably a beautiful lawn. As Laurel and I ride up the sidewalk to the two-story brick building, all is quiet. But a pile of goo on the sidewalk outside the custodians' office leads me to fear that pigs have traveled where no pigs have gone before.

"Watch out," I warn Laurel as she stops her bike, her

foot landing about a centimeter to the left of the pile.

"Crap!" She does a little two-step to avoid it.

"That would be my guess. Let's prop our bikes in that cubbyhole."

Now that we're here, I have no idea what to do. Skirting the pile of goo—and keeping an eye out for others—I try the custodians' door. The knob turns, which is surprising since I expected Ferret and his crew to lock up behind themselves.

As I pull the door open, I tell Laurel, "Make sure Carmine doesn't get in behind us." Before I finish my sentence, he shoves past my leg into the building. After a sprawling takeoff on the slippery tile floor, he skids down the hall and out of sight.

"No, Carmine!" I call. "Come here, Carmine!"

Beside me, Laurel watches him disappear. "Your dog can move! The only time I was that excited about being in school was freshman year back in Evanston. Our drama teacher came to first period with three hickeys on his neck. I sneaked his picture with my cell during class and posted it on Facebook." She nods and smiles. "Now, that was educational."

Inside the building there's an odor that reeks of barn yard. I'm used to smelling cafeteria food and jock straps moldering on locker shelves, but this is much worse. The air—damp, heavy, and still—intensifies the stench.

Emergency lights in the ceiling create alternating sections of dark and light reflecting off the rows of lockers in the hallway. Everything is quiet. "The pigs are probably shut in Hammond's office," Laurel whispers as she starts toward the main office, which is halfway down the hall on our right.

One floor above us, I hear a series of barks followed by a chorus of high-pitched squeals and the clatter of hooves.

"Or not." I jog toward the stairway. My flip-flops buckle under my feet, so I yank them off and toss them into a corner. Taking the steps two at the time, Laurel and I race to the second-floor landing. We bump fists for luck and push through the swinging double doors into the hallway.

There we find ourselves nose to snout with three wild-eyed, not-so-little pigs. Like flightless geese on steroids, they're rumbling toward us in V formation, their chunky bratwurst bodies waddling from side to side. Carmine nips at their hooves in a howling, barking frenzy.

Laurel dives across the hall into a recessed doorway. I retreat through the swinging doors, slip in a puddle of pig poop, and clutch the stair rail with both hands. For a second, my feet touch nothing but air. Then I grip the edge of the top step and pull myself to safety. For the first time in my life, I'm thankful for my freakishly long toes.

For one traitorous second, I consider leaving Laurel,

Carmine, and the pigs to work things out among themselves. But I wouldn't be able to forgive myself for the few hours I'd survive before Laurel hunted me down and killed me.

My left foot is greasy with pig crap, and my first step nearly lands me on my butt. I look around for something to wipe it on, but there's nothing but tile and brick.

"Aspen, I need you! Get in here!" Laurel shrieks.

Taking shallow breaths—the smell of pig waste has put me off deep breathing—I push through the double doors. Poor Laurel is pancaked in the doorway on the other side of the hall. With her hands and feet braced on either side of the doorframe, she's trying to suspend herself off the floor. Directly under her, the pigs are being held captive by Carmine. Their hooves scrabble on the slippery floor as they try to shove their way through the closed door. Their piercing squeals are making my ears ache.

Laurel's face is the color of the brick wall, and her arm muscles are quivering. "Do something!"

If I think about what I'm going to do, I won't. Barefoot, my teeth gritted, I wade into the whirlpool of pigs and dog. Overheated pig flanks crash into my knees, and I hug the wall for support. If I go down, there's a better than even chance I won't get up.

I zero in on Carmine, who is panting and frothing at the mouth. I straddle him like a bow-legged cowboy

31

and clamp onto his back with my knees. With both hands holding his collar, I haul him back with all my strength.

He doesn't budge.

Based on our many dog-walking fiascos, I know how much harder Carmine pulls than I do, but I was hoping adrenaline would give me an edge. Unfortunately Carmine is drooling adrenaline, and he has the advantages of four-legged traction and actual muscle mass.

"Carmine, come. Be a good boy." His eyes roll in my direction, which means he's hoping for a reward. Since he has a year's supply of food within inches of his mouth, that can't be it. Carmine eyes me again. His sides are heaving, and his tongue is hanging halfway to the floor.

"Are you thirsty, boy? Want a drink of water?"

When Carmine turns his head toward me, I know I've got him. Holding his collar and gurgling baby talk, I lead him down the hall to the drinking fountains. With my hip I push the rectangular button on the front of the wheelchair accessible fountain. As soon as Carmine sees the water, he stands on his hind legs and slurps.

Now that Carmine isn't holding the pigs hostage, they shuffle away from Laurel. Freed from the doorway, she hurries over just in time to see Carmine running his tongue all over the bottom of the fountain. "My God, Aspen! The people who drink that water have enough problems without having to deal with dog slobber!"

As if dog drool in the basin of the water cooler is our biggest sanitary issue tonight. "If we survive this ordeal, I'll disinfect it."

Carmine is straining toward the spouting water, and I wrestle him back. It's not coming out fast enough for him and he's looking for a way to climb in. "Find a container we can fill with water, or tomorrow people will be drinking where a dog's butt has been!"

"Eeuw!" Laurel covers her mouth. She looks up and down the hall as if waiting for a parade of dog dishes to march past. "Where can we get a water bowl?"

Holding Carmine back is making my shoulders ache, and the smell of hot, drooling dog and pig crap has my stomach bucking like a wild horse. "Let's think. You're standing by the teachers' lounge where they drink liquids like coffee in . . . what do they call those things? Oh, yeah, coffee cups. Might that be a place to look?" I suggest in my most patient, reasonable voice.

"There's no need to get nasty!" Laurel gives me her spooky, one-eyed glare before she opens the door to the teachers' lounge.

Keeping a death grip on Carmine's collar, I check to make sure the pigs aren't planning an attack. They're grouped at the end of the hall staring at me with their piggy little eyes. Their huge, flappy pink ears wave like palm leaves, and their flat snouts are splattered with black

Dalmatian-type spots. They're actually cute in a pre–pork chop kind of way.

Laurel opens the door and sticks her head out. "Good news, Aspen! There's a unisex bathroom in here. Carmine can drink toilet water until he explodes."

"You hear that, Carmine?" I tell him. "Lots of water!" Laurel holds the door open, and I lead Carmine in. When he sees the toilet, he springs at it and sticks his head in the bowl. I wag my head toward the hall, and Laurel and I slip out. The lounge door opens inward, so no matter how hard Carmine shoves, he's trapped.

"An excellent idea," I tell Laurel. "Now all we have to do is get the pigs outside."

"Yeah, that's all we have to do," Laurel says with more sarcasm than necessary, considering she got us into this mess. She cups her hands around her mouth. "Hey, pigs, the coast is clear!" she calls. "Time to hit the road!"

"Very funny. Cut back on the attitude, Pork Queen, or I'll leave you to deal with the Snout Sisters by yourself."

Laurel shoves her sweaty bangs out of her eyes. "How do you know they're sisters? They could be guy pigs."

"You are such a city girl." Although this is the only time outside of the Iowa State Fair I've seen a pig in person.

"If you know so much, then answer me." Laurel peers at me under her lowered eyelids.

The best defense is slinging a load of bull. "What are

you, a sex ed dropout? Guy animals have penises; those pigs don't. End of discussion." I can't believe we're outside the teachers' lounge at one thirty in the morning arguing over pig genitals.

"I never knew you were such a perv!" Laurel hoots. "I'm trying to avoid being trampled by wild killer pigs and you're checking them for penises. Gross!"

After I get Laurel off the subject of pig parts, we review our predicament. Now that Carmine is trapped in the lounge, the pigs are showing an unseemly interest in us. Their mouths are open, and they're snuffling toward us at an alarming pace. I'm pretty sure one of them is salivating.

"Do pigs bite?" Laurel asks. She ducks behind me and watches their approach over my shoulder.

A quick sidestep puts me behind her. "How should I know? My dad's an insurance agent, not Old MacDonald."

Laurel tries to get around me again, but I block her with my elbow. "They're still coming. What should we do?"

When did I become the freaking pig guru? "They look hungry. Hold out your arm and see what they do."

Carmine woofs from inside the teachers' lounge, and Laurel's eyes light up. "Wait. Carmine was more inter-ested in water than food. The pigs probably are, too!" She pounds my shoulder, knocking me against the wall.

"Think about it. The poor things were pig-napped and shoved up a flight of stairs. Then Carmine chased them all over the place. They're probably dying of thirst."

Laurel's moods shift at mind-blowing speed. Two minutes ago these were wild killer pigs. Now she's feeling sorry for them. But a good idea is a good idea. "If I'm right—and I know I am—we just fill a container with water," she continues, "and our three bacon bits follow it right out the door."

A flashbulb goes off in my brain. "Or right into the elevator, which has to be easier than persuading them to walk down the steps."

I leave Laurel minding the pigs while I raid the lounge for water containers. Now that I'm not wrestling Carmine, I notice that the lounge is cramped and dingy with walls the same yellowish brown as the pig deposits on the floor outside. In the middle of the room is a scarred-up table surrounded by eight mismatched cafeteria chairs. A refrigerator older than my grandmother stands beside the bathroom door. Carmine is stretched out on a sagging couch with his head on the arm nearest the door. When I walk in, he opens his eyes and yawns.

"Go back to sleep, troublemaker." Carmine groans and his eyes droop shut. Why doesn't he obey like that when I ask him to do something important?

At least I don't have to waste time looking for a water

bowl. A stainless-steel bowl half-filled with popcorn is sitting on the countertop beside the sink. As I pick it up, three cockroaches—one of them bigger than my thumb—scamper out of the leftovers. They dive over the rim of the bowl and disappear into the crack between the counter and the wall.

My teeth clench against a scream. Pig poop and cockroaches. What's next? Holding the bowl with two fingers, I prepare to dump the bug-ridden popcorn into the trash can. Then I stop. Maybe the pigs are hungry. A few cockroaches won't bother them. I find a grocery sack under the sink, pour in the popcorn, and fill the greasy bowl with water.

With the sack crushed in my armpit and holding the bowl of water in both hands, I lurch back into the hall. "Make way for Aspen Parks, caterer to the stars. I don't like to brag, but my clients include Miss Piggy, Porky, Wilbur, and Piglet, just to name a few!"

"Shh! Not so loud. I just got them calmed down." Laurel leans against the wall, rubbing one of the pigs on the snout and scratching another behind the ears. The third one is snuffling her leg. "Come here and touch them. They feel all warm and bristly."

The skin between my shoulder blades bunches up. "Uh, maybe later. I've got water and popcorn. Let's see if they'll follow us to the elevator."

"Do you hear that?" Laurel coos. "Popcorn *and* water! Yummy!"

I hold the popcorn sack at arm's length. "Here, pigs. Popcorn. Good stuff."

Their heads swivel toward me, their ears perk up, and their blocky heads bob up and down. The next thing I know, six beady eyes are trained on me, and the grunting, snuffling trio of pigs is closing in fast. I hand the popcorn off to Laurel and hold the water down where they can see it.

"Show time, Laurel," I say from the corner of my mouth.

We shuffle backward toward the elevator with the pigs hot on our toes. To keep them interested, Laurel scatters popcorn kernels along the way. The pigs vacuum up the corn without breaking stride and keep on coming. I reach back and push the elevator button without taking my eyes off them. Who knows what a hungry pig might find appetizing?

When the doors slide apart, I set the bowl of greasy water on the floor and back out in a hurry. "Toss the popcorn inside," I tell Laurel. "Then we close the doors and let them out on the first floor."

"We can't leave them alone in the elevator!" Laurel says. "They'll be scared."

I rub my aching temples. "Fine. Keep your new friends company. I'll meet you downstairs."

Laurel steps to the back of the elevator and shakes the popcorn bag. "Come on, girls. Go for a ride with Aunt Laurel." The pigs troop in with her, and she pushes the button.

That girl is in serious need of a pet.

I sprint down the stairs to the first floor, but Laurel and the pigs are already waiting for me in the hall outside Principal Hammond's office. The pigs are rooting for old maids in the torn grocery bag, and Laurel is patting one of them on the back. "Rose and Daisy liked the elevator, but Sunflower here seemed nervous. Weren't you, baby girl?"

Laurel rests her hand on Sunflower's head. "I wuz scared, Auntie Laurel." Laurel's lips barely move and the gravely, baby-talk voice sounds nothing like her. "But you made me feel all better. I wuv you."

My neck hairs prickle. Laurel's teacher impersonations are amazing, but her pig-channeling routine is spooky. I'm half expecting "Auntie Laurel" to sling a leg over Sunflower's back and ride off into the sunrise. Seeing this side of her leaves me feeling unsettled, like last year when a bunch of us went to Hooters after a basketball game and saw the school librarian waiting tables.

"This is great. Now we just set them free, and we can go home." Laurel is scratching Daisy's cheek. Or maybe that's Rose. "Being a good citizen is exhausting."

"We can't just turn them loose on the street, you know."

Laurel gives me a blank look. Then she rubs her eyes with her pig-scratching hand, and the glazed look clears. "God, of course not! They might get lost or hit by a car. What are we going to do?"

I let out a defeated sigh. "The one thing I wanted to avoid at all costs. I'll have to call Manny." I pat my shorts looking for my cell phone and discover two problems. First, my gym shorts don't have pockets. Second, my phone is at home on my bed. "Let me use your cell."

"No freaking way!" Laurel shouts, causing the pigs to do a nervous shuffle that's dangerously close to my bare toes. "Manny can't see me like this. My hair is a mess, and I haven't brushed my teeth." She holds her hand up to her mouth and breathes on it. "My breath smells awful!"

Pigs have been rubbing against her, and a chunk of poop is stuck on top of her left shoe, but yeah, her breath is the big issue. "Come on, Manny won't even . . ." I haven't yet found a kind way to tell Laurel that yearning after my brother is a waste of time. Manny likes his girls tall, slutty, and really busty. If his selection process goes beyond that, I haven't seen evidence of it.

But Laurel's not listening to me anyway. "Can't we call somebody else?"

"Like who? A pig chauffeur?" I throw my hands up in frustration. "Our choices are your dad, my parents, or Manny. You choose."

"You've lived here your whole life, and you don't know anybody who has a pickup?"

"Some of my parents' friends, maybe. And, of course, there's Buster. I'm sure he'd be thrilled to drive back here and pick up the very same pigs he dumped off. We could get Ferret and Kong to help us load them up."

Laurel sighs and hands over her phone.

Manny answers the third time I call. "Laurel, quit calling," he mumbles. "This isn't Aspen's phone."

"Don't hang up! It's Aspen. Laurel and I have a situation." I explain in as few words as possible, surprised at Manny's low-key reaction—until I hear the snore. "Manny, wake up! Laurel and I are being held hostage at the high school! It's life or death!"

"Then call the police." The last word is muffled by a yawn.

"Listen, Manfred, I blew my weekend busting my ass for your graduation party. If you're not here in ten minutes, I'm telling Mom what you did Saturday night."

"Keep your shorts on. I'm coming."

"So what did he do Saturday night?" Laurel wants to know when I close the phone.

"I wish I knew. After tonight, I'm going to need some major leverage."

I'm waiting in the parking lot when Manny coasts in, after cutting his lights a block away. I step up to the driver's

41

side, and he powers down the window. "This better be serious."

Pig tales don't lend themselves to sugarcoating, so I lay out the facts. The further I get into the story, the lower Manny sinks in his seat. After I finish, he's so still that I wonder if he's asleep with his eyes open. Then his head moves slowly from side to side. "So right this minute, your friend Laurel and three medium-size pigs are standing outside Hammond's office?" I nod. "And what am I supposed to do about it?"

"Well, the pigs aren't *that* big. I thought maybe the three of us could lift them into your trunk—"

Manny explodes out of his car. "No way are pigs coming near my car! I just spent a hundred and fifty bucks to have this baby detailed." He lays his hand protectively on the roof.

I sort of knew he was going to say that. "Look, Manny, if we don't get the pigs out of here, Laurel and I will be suspended—probably worse."

"And how is that my problem?"

"Laurel and I don't have transportation, so it's only logical for people to think you were in on it. Laurel may even have mentioned your name on her Facebook page. Think how upset Mom and Dad will be when you're banned from graduation."

Manny's jaw works back and forth, grinding the enamel off his teeth. "Show me."

Laurel's sitting against the wall with her legs stretched out. The pigs are lying on either side of her, asleep. She puts her fingers to her lips.

"Not that big?" Manny growls. "They're half grown." He walks away, shaking his head. But he flips open his phone and makes a call.

I step over a snoring pig and settle in next to Laurel. "Who's he calling?" she whispers. I shrug, lean my head on the wall, and close my eyes. The next thing I know, Laurel is poking my shoulder. "Aspen, wake up. Manny's friend with the truck is here."

"Good." I wipe the drool from my chin and push myself to a standing position. Some stray hairs on the back of my head snag on the brick wall, and I yank them free. "Let's get this show on the road so I can go home and sleep."

I'm slumped against the wall, rubbing my eyes and yawning, when a deep voice says, "They're here all right, just like you said—pigs at Cottonwood Creek High."

My eyes pop open. Beside Manny is a tall guy wearing jeans and a green flannel shirt. His hair is dark reddish brown, and the freckled forearms sticking out of his rolled-up sleeves are packed with muscle. When he sees me checking him out, his face flushes.

"I was referring to the four-legged animals, not you girls," he says.

Laurel gets to her feet. "And we appreciate it."

I'd like to say something clever, but my tongue is paralyzed. For no rational reason, I've always been magnetically attracted to red-haired guys. And this guy is way more than a redhead. He's tall and built and—okay, maybe he's not exactly handsome. Wait, that's not true. He is exactly handsome. From ten feet away I can see the electric blue of his eyes. All of that put together makes him the Superman of redheads.

"Clay, that's Laurel, my sister's best friend," Manny says. "And the mute holding up the wall is my sister, Aspen."

Clay nods. "Nice to meet you both. Great names, too. Outdoorsy." To keep my eyes from meeting his, I watch my feet as I step out of the Magic Circle of Pigs.

"Okay. This should be easy." Clay steps to the nearest pig and taps her shoulder. "Up, pig." His voice is firm but calm. I wouldn't mind having his hand on my shoulder— or other select locations, for that matter.

The pig must be familiar with that command because she grunts and pushes herself up.

"That one's Sunflower," Laurel tells him. "These two are Rose and Daisy."

Clay cuts her a puzzled look. "I wasn't aware that Dale Crawford named his pigs. As far as I know, the notches in their ears are as far as he goes toward identification."

Laurel rests her hands on her hips. "Those are the names Aspen and I gave them."

How did I get involved in this?

"They're all girls, aren't they?" she asks.

"Human females are girls." Clay thumps Rose's flank, and she stands, too. "Female pigs are gilts until they have piglets. After they farrow they're called sows." He repeats the tapping process with Daisy. "These three are too young to breed."

"You hear that, Aspen? We're not the only virgins at Cottonwood Creek High after all." Laurel giggles at her own humor.

Manny barks out a laugh, and I look for a place to hide.

"Okay then," Clay says, wisely choosing not to respond. Now that all three pigs are standing, he taps Sunflower behind the left shoulder. She slowly rotates until her face is pointing toward the side door. "You never hit a pig on the rump. All they need is a tap on the flank to let them know which direction to head."

Laurel walks to the pig on Clay's left and taps its flank. She turns toward the door. "Come on, Aspen. You guide Daisy. This is cool."

I glance at Manny, who shakes his head. "She's all yours, Sis."

What am I worried about? I've seen how tame they are.

I walk to Daisy and poke her in the side with my index finger. Her bristles feel like the brush Dad uses to clean the grill. She looks at me from the corner of her eye, but she doesn't move. Clay and Laurel's pigs are shuffling down the hall, leaving Daisy and me behind. If I can't do this simple thing, Clay will think I'm a loser.

"Come on, Daisy," I whisper near her ear. "Help a girl out." This time I poke her with two fingers. With a grunt, she follows Sunflower and Rose. In his usual helpful way, Manny props his elbow on a glass display case and smirks as Daisy and I plod past.

As I catch up to Clay and Laurel, Clay says, "You two are naturals. If you get bored this summer, you can come out and help me on the farm."

"What do you raise?" Laurel asks. My tongue locks up around cute guys, but she can make conversation with anyone.

"I'm experimenting with nontraditional crops. I've planted thirty acres with amaranth, and I've got a hundred acres in prairie seed." Clay looks over his shoulder to include me in his answer. "It's a renewable crop that's great for the environment, especially here in Iowa. With global warming on everyone's mind, prairie restoration is skyrocketing. On the downside, seed harvesting is incredibly demanding, but . . ."

Clay's handsome, built, and environmentally aware. He couldn't be more my type if I'd ordered him online. My mind is drifting to our romantic first date when it dawns on me that he's stopped talking midsentence.

"Sorry. Pretty boring, huh?" Clay says with an apologetic smile. Behind him, Laurel is sending frantic eye signals while pointing at her wide-open mouth.

Which is when I realize my mouth is gaping open in a rude, jaw-stretching yawn. "No, I'm not . . ."

But Clay is telling Manny to hold the door open, and I'm looking at Sunflower's rump as Clay guides her out. Laurel leaves Rose long enough to hiss, "Why were you yawning? Clay is totally your type."

Exhaustion and sleep-deprivation are two reasons that come to mind.

Clay comes back through the door. "One in the truck. Two to go." With Clay and Laurel on either side of Rose, she trots out, too.

As they walk out, I hear Laurel ask, "What keeps Sunflower from jumping out of the truck while you're in here?"

"I just close the tailgate," Clay says. "No pig is going to jump over that."

While I've been busy humiliating myself, Daisy has shuffled a few feet away. I walk over to tap her to the exit. "Don't go wild on me now. Girls in our situation have a—"

"What situation is that?" Without making a sound Clay has come up next to me, so close that his breath warms my neck. Shouldn't he be wearing those loud, clunky farmer boots?

"The being exhausted situation," I manage without stammering. "I've spent the weekend getting the house ready for Manny's graduation party. And Daisy here is worn out from trying to adjust to the high school experience."

Clay smiles. No dimples, but he doesn't need them. "Are you saying my prairie seed monologue wasn't the reason you yawned?"

"No. I mean, yes." Now I'm back to my usual self. "I mean, I'm totally interested in environmental issues, prairie restoration, and all that nature stuff."

"Gotcha." Clay touches two fingers to his eyebrow in a salute. "Then let's get Daisy loaded into my truck so all the virgins can go home to bed."

If humiliation can kill, I'm a dead woman.

I stay a few steps behind while Clay persuades Daisy out of the building. Laurel and I scratch her ears while he lowers the pickup's tailgate and props a wooden ramp against it. With a tap on Daisy's side, he coaxes her up the ramp to the bed of his pickup, where Sunflower and Rose are standing. He detaches the ramp, slides it in beside the pigs, and slams the tailgate shut with practiced ease. He opens the driver's-side door, and I have to hold on to the flagpole to keep from diving into the cab with him.

"Nice meeting you, Laurel—Aspen." In the dark it's hard to tell, but I imagine Clay is gazing at me with longing. "And, Manny, it's been an interesting experience. See you next weekend at the golf course."

Then, in a haze of dust and lingering pig odor, the guy of my dreams drives out of my life.

five

AS WE WALK BACK INSIDE THE SCHOOL, LAUREL BRUSHES HER palms together. "Well, I'm glad that's over. Let's get our stuff and go home. I could sleep for a week."

"At least." I yawn so wide it hurts. As I wander over to the bottom of the stairs to pick up my flip-flops, I hear a muffled howl floating down from the second floor. "Crud! I forgot about Carmine."

"Carmine's not all you forgot," Manny says in his superior older brother voice.

"Nice try, bro." I pause with my left foot on the bottom step. "Three pigs came in, three pigs went out. Case closed."

Manny chuckles. "But they left numerous reminders

of their time at Cottonwood Creek High." He nods at a yellowish pile in front of the office.

I press the heels of my hands into my skull. "Crap, crap, crap!"

"You're right about that, Sis." Manny hitches up his baggy shorts. "You girls better clean up this mess before the custodian gets here at five thirty."

Laurel sidles up to Manny with a smile I'm sure she thinks is sexy, but the mascara streaks under her eyes kind of ruin the effect. "If you helped us, we'd get done a lot faster."

"You're probably right, but I'm going to take a nap in my car. Wake me up when you finish so I can make sure you get home okay."

Laurel's eyes follow Manny as he walks away scratching his butt. "I think your brother's finally starting to notice me."

"It's probably the pig poop in your hair." I rub my eyes. "Since I've got to let Carmine out of the lounge before he scratches the door to shreds, we might as well start upstairs."

Laurel picks up the mostly empty water bowl and chucks the torn popcorn sack into a trash can. Then she follows me up the steps. On our way to the lounge, we scout out pig piles. We count seven on the second floor, which is at least a dozen too many.

I try to push open the lounge door to let Carmine out,

but he keeps lunging against it and doesn't listen when I try to explain about doors that open in versus those that open out. Finally, Laurel and I use our combined weight to overpower him. As soon as Carmine sees daylight, he wedges through the opening and disappears through the swinging doors at the top of the stairs.

"You're welcome!" Laurel calls after him. She walks in and sets the bowl by the sink. "Do you think I should wash it?"

I shake my head. "It was full of rancid popcorn and cockroaches. Pig spit seems like an improvement." Something swishes around my feet, and I realize the floor is ankle-deep with shredded toilet paper.

Laurel notices, too. "Looks like Carmine got bored. I wonder how many rolls he went through."

I sigh. "As many as he could find."

After Laurel and I pick up the TP and stuff it into a trash can in the hall outside the lounge, we raid the custodians' closet for cleaning supplies. Even if you ignored the gross, mushy texture and putrid smell, pig poo would still be the most disgusting substance on the planet. Which makes gag control a priority.

To prevent a major puke outbreak, we try to distract ourselves by talking. As I wring another mop-full into the custodians' rolling bucket, I ask, "So, you're a pig lover. How long has that been going on?"

Laurel wipes her sweaty forehead with the back of her hand. "It's not just pigs. I'm wild about all animals—cows, koalas, hyenas, whatever."

"Why don't you have a pet?"

"Allergies—Mom's and Dad's, not mine." Laurel's mop slaps the floor. "They swell up like dirigibles when they're near anything with fur. It's a mystery how I avoided it."

"That's too bad." Carmine is a pain in my rear, but he's like the sweet, loving brother I never had.

Laurel shrugs. "I've gotten used to it. In a couple of years I'll be able to have all the pets I want. Until then, I stick with temporary, random pets like my new friends the pig triplets."

Whatever works, I guess. "Now that you have pig friends, are you going vegetarian?"

Laurel cocks her head to one side. "Why would I do that?"

"Well, you don't want to end up eating one of your new girlfriends."

She laughs. "I was worried about that, too, so I asked Clay while we were helping Rose into the truck. He said the girls would be fine. Female pigs spend their lives eating, sleeping, and having piglets. And when they get too old to have babies, they're put out to pasture. Just the males get eaten."

Only a big-city girl would believe that fairy tale, but

Clay told that story so Laurel would feel better, which makes me like him even more.

"So they're like my great-aunt Evelyn," Laurel says. "She and Great-uncle Cecil had sixteen kids. He died, and now she spends all her time playing canasta and going on cruises."

"I see." I'm not going to ruin her fantasy. "Well, we're finished up here. Let's see if your new friends left us anything on the first floor."

A few minutes after three a.m. we dump the last of the pig goop water into the utility sink and replace the mops and buckets. Laurel grabs her hoodie from where she hung it on the office doorknob, and we drag our limp bodies out to the parking lot. The pile of poop outside the door is a squashed mess, and we decide to leave it.

The driver's seat of Manny's car is reclined all the way back, and he's leaned against the door with his mouth hanging open. No wonder Laurel finds him irresistible.

With my fists clenched, I pound on the window above his head. He bolts awake, bumping his head against the steering wheel. I wiggle my fingers in greeting, and he sticks up one of his.

"All done," I say through the window. "We're ready for a ride home. Pop the trunk and we'll load up our bikes."

He powers the window down an inch or so. "Are you insane? You're not tracking pig crap into my car."

54

I tug on the door handle, but it's locked. "But you said—"

"I said I'd make sure you got home okay. And I will." Manny moves his seat back to vertical. "You pedal; I'll follow. Safe as can be."

I am so using his golf letter jacket the next time I dust the furniture.

Since Laurel's house is on the way to ours, we go there first. I'm almost too tired to gag when she gets all gushy thanking Manny for helping us.

At home Manny parks on the slab beside our garage and waits while I put my bike away. When I move into smelling range, he holds his nose. "Holy crap! You smell worse than the pigs! You'd better shower before you go to bed."

"Thanks for your concern about my hygiene. You don't mind if I roll on your bedroom rug a few times first?"

He yawns. "Go for it. Just do it quietly."

I yawn back. "I'm not sure I have the energy to climb the stairs." I unhook the gate. My sweat cools as we walk through our pitch-black backyard, and I shiver.

Manny unlocks the kitchen door and lets me in first. Except for the humming refrigerator, the house is quiet. As in no Carmine jumping on us at the door.

"Carmine's not here. Suppose he got lost?"

"Are you kidding?" Manny pulls grapefruit juice from

the fridge. "When you girls were cleaning up, he blasted out of the side door and raced toward home at about fifty miles per hour. I'll bet you a hundred bucks he's asleep on your bed."

By the dog door are muddy pawprints leading upstairs. I point them out to Manny. "You're right. There's the evidence."

"Problem solved." He sets the empty juice carton in the sink. "See you in a few hours."

"Too few." As he's walking out of the kitchen, I add, "Thanks. Seriously."

He waves and heads upstairs.

I lock the back door and head for bed. As Manny predicted, Carmine is sprawled crosswise on my bed like a cheap bearskin rug. I kick off my flip-flops, shove him to one side, and sink into unconsciousness.

Six

"ASPEN, WHY ARE YOU STILL IN BED? YOU'RE SUPPOSED TO BE at school in fifteen minutes!" Dad roars from the hallway, yanking me from dreamland.

I reach out blindly and pull a pillow over my head. I just crawled into bed. It can't be time to get up yet.

He tosses the pillow onto the floor. "Come on, Sprout. You can do it. Only a couple more weeks to go."

I roll onto my back. Dad's face is pink and shiny and what's left of his hair is wet from the shower. His mint green polo shirt and khaki slacks don't have a wrinkle. How can an old dude like Dad look all fresh and alert in the morning when I feel like roadkill? "Two weeks and three days. It's a lifetime."

"Speaking of life," Dad says with a frown, "it smells like something died in here. Not recently, either." He sniffs near Carmine, who is still doing his rug impersonation on my bed. "Phew! He found something extra ripe to roll in this time!"

Dad ruffles Carmine's ears and tugs on his collar until his eyes open. "Come on, buddy. You're exiled to the backyard until somebody has time to give you a bath." He leads Carmine to the door.

"Here's the deal. If you're downstairs in ten minutes, I'll give you a ride," Dad says on his way out.

When he's gone I pull my mud- and poop-covered feet out from under the covers. The stench makes my eyes water. As I race for the shower, I silently apologize to Carmine for letting him take a bum rap. After school I'll splash a little water on him so he looks like he's had a bath and take him for an extra long walk to make up for it.

Dad drops me at the corner to avoid the chaos in the school parking lot. I scan the area for Laurel and see her waving from the cubby in the wall where we stashed our bikes last night. This morning. Whenever. My brain is foggier than Manny's windows last winter when he and Cynthia parked in our driveway.

When I'm within striking distance of Laurel, she grabs my arm and drags me into the cubby. If she keeps up the arm grabbing, her fingerprints will be embedded in my skin.

As if carving trenches in my flesh isn't enough, she shakes me. My limp arm flops like an overstretched rubber band. "We forgot to clean the elevator! And I'm pretty sure Rose had an accident on the way down."

I yawn and rub my grainy eyes with my free hand. "There's nothing we can do about it now, and I'm too wiped out to care. Who's going to notice on a Monday morning, anyway?"

"But—"

"But nothing." I pry Laurel's fingers loose and shake the blood back into my arm. "Unless they call in CSI to do an analysis, nobody will know what's in that pile. I guarantee that the custodian's not going to give it the sniff test before he mops."

"You're right." Laurel sighs. "I guess I'm too tired to think straight."

I slump against the wall. "That makes two of us."

A hulking shadow blocks the sun. "There are two of you, all right," a high-pitched male voice mocks. "Two major losers asking to get their faces busted open." After delivering the line that earned him his nickname, Buster Reese exposes the tobacco wad in his cheek in a brown-toothed sneer. With his tattooed arms crossed over his beefy chest and his flabby stomach almost sucked in, I'm sure he strikes terror into the hearts of children under ten.

Okay, maybe he scares me, too. Ferret is disgusting and annoying, but Buster is pure evil. From reading the police calls section of the *Cottonwood Creek Gazette* I know Buster's been busted for vandalism, assault, criminal mischief, and public intoxication. I've heard rumors that he's done a lot worse, and the crap he pulls at school is enough to convince me. I've seen him trip guys and elbow them in the gut just because they're within reach. Girls walk to class in pairs as protection against Buster cornering them in the stairwell for his idea of romance. Two weeks ago he aimed his truck at a squirrel crossing the street. I wouldn't be surprised if he goes after small children, too.

"Yeah, busted open," Kong Chesterfield chimes in, punching his meaty right fist into the palm of his left hand. Having reached his conversational limit, Kong stops palm-punching to swat at a swarm of early-rising gnats.

Laurel and I catch each other's eyes, and my uneasiness comes out in a giggle. Kong's nickname came from his monstrous size, sloping forehead, and inept ball handling on the basketball court. Buster is close to six feet tall, but the top of his head barely reaches Kong's chin. Kong has never looked more like King Kong swiping at planes in his signature death scene than he does now.

Ferret pokes his head under Kong's armpit. "What are you laughing at, Ash Rot?"

Laurel lifts her chin. "Look in a mirror, Ferret, and you won't have to ask."

Buster spits a stream of tobacco on the sidewalk. "Quit trying to distraction us, bitches. We know what you did."

I pull up a confused frown, which isn't difficult. Buster has four-letter words mastered. If he ventures beyond that, you'll need an interpreter. But he's also infamous for slamming guys into their lockers because they *might* be looking at him funny. Which means I keep my mouth shut.

"As usual, I have no idea what you're talking about, Buster." Laurel bats her lashes in wide-eyed innocence, which totally works—with her left eye. The right one looks a little guilty.

"Cut the crap," Ferret says. "Last night we went to a lot of trouble to pull off the most awesome stunt in this loser school's history. And it went off smooth as snot."

Not the best choice of words for a guy with chronic booger issues.

"We got everybody here early to watch Hammond walk into a mess of pigs." Ferret gestures at the crowd of before-school loiterers, which—now that I notice—is larger than usual.

With my hand half-covering my mouth, I mutter, "A herd."

"What?" Ferret shoves a wad of greasy hair behind his oddly tiny ear.

I lower my hand. "A group of pigs is called a herd, not a mess."

Kong scratches his armpit. "It was supposed to be pigs and a mess," he observes.

Ferret gives him a look that's half-frown, half-disbelief. "So the senior class is here bright and early to see Hammond get trampled by the three little pigs, and what do they see?"

"An exceptionally lovely sunrise?" Laurel suggests.

"Nothing," Ferret snarls. "No pig crap, no pigs, no nothing."

Buster shifts his chaw to his other cheek. "Which makes us three look bad in front of all our friends."

Does the guy have a clue how many ways Laurel could go with that comment? Before she opens her mouth, I give her the "Don't You Dare Say What You're Thinking" look.

A smile creeps across Kong's face. "Except there is pigs, Buster. They're right here in front of us."

Ferret snorts with laughter. It takes Buster a few beats longer to get the joke. Then he claps Kong on the back. "You're right, buddy. But nobody's interested in looking at their ugly faces."

I shift my American history text to my right hand. Maybe I couldn't get all three of them, but I could shorten Ferret's nose by a couple of inches before Buster flattened me.

Laurel beats me to it. She pulls a can of pepper spray

from her purse and aims it at Buster. "You butt crusts have brightened our morning, but now it's time for you to go. Walk away by the time I count three, or you'll be spitting pepper for a week."

Buster puffs out his chest. "Come on, guys. Let's get outta here before people start thinking we're with these bitches."

Bile rises in the back of my throat. Cissy Russell told half the junior girls that Buster tried to rape her at a party last winter. Being "with him" is close to the worst thing I can imagine.

Buster spews a gob of tobacco at our feet. Laurel and I jump apart, but brown drops land on our bare toes. My stomach tries to turn itself inside out, and I'm grateful I didn't have time for breakfast.

Buster swaggers away with Kong knuckle-dragging in his wake. Ferret lags behind. Buster is their evil leader, Ferret's the oversize mouth, and Kong is the brainless muscle. Put them together and you've got a swaggering, foul-mouthed, bullying Buttferk.

"This isn't the end of it." Ferret raises his upper lip to show off his pointed little teeth. "You can't mess us up like that and get away with it."

"Oh, I'm pretty sure we can," Laurel counters. "Your parents made a mess of you, and nothing happened to them."

I clear my throat. "Well, actually, something did happen to Ferret's parents. They got saddled with him for the rest of their lives."

"Excellent, Aspen!" Laurel and I bump fists.

Ferret's so mad his eyes are crossing. "Laugh it up, tree scabs. But when my buds and I decide all the ways we're going to get even, we'll see who's laughing." He favors us with a parting snarl before he turns and hurries after Buster and Kong.

I watch him go with a queasy feeling in my stomach. "So, do you really think Buttferk will be out for revenge?"

"If they are, I hope Ferret posts their plans on Facebook." Laurel sends a puff of air into her bangs. "Being stalked is exactly the kind of drama we need to get us noticed."

"Yeah, I'm hoping for that, too. When the police find our bloody corpses, they'll just check your news feed and know exactly who to arrest."

Don't ask me how the morning passes. I shuffle from class to class in a sleep-deprived haze. The absolute second I get home, I'm going to hit my bed and not move a muscle until tomorrow.

Which makes this the worst possible day to have gym class.

Normally I don't mind gym, although I'm required

to gripe about it like everyone else. We're two weeks into an archery unit, which—in spite of my stringy arms—I don't suck at. But a person in my semi-comatose condition should not be wielding anything that resembles a lethal weapon. Laurel and I hang at the end of the line of shooters, where we plan to stay until the period ends.

Eyes closed, my face lifted to the warm sunshine, I'm wondering if it's possible to sleep standing up. I scoot my feet apart for balance and let myself sway from side to side. *I'm lying in a hammock by the ocean, letting the gentle salt breeze rock—*

"God, Aspen, you look like Death's ugly stepchild. I mean it. I bet the Grim Reaper has lighter circles under his eyes."

So much for the ocean breeze. When I open my eyes, Laurel is studying me with a horrified expression. "Thanks, Laurel. I thought I couldn't possibly feel worse, but you just pushed me past that barrier."

"Hey, Piedmont, come here." Tessa Chandler, one of Cottonwood Creek's party girls, hooks a thumb at Laurel. She's lounging on the grass under a tree, filing her nails. "We need to talk." Tessa's the only high school student—male or female—with smaller boobs than mine. That should make her one of my favorite people, but it doesn't.

Laurel nudges me, and we head over.

"Not her, just you," says Tessa's best friend, Wynter

Green. People make fun of my name, but they let her slide. Just shows how much you can get away with if you're popular.

Laurel stops in her tracks. "No thanks. If you want to talk to me, Aspen comes, too."

Tessa and Wynter look at each other with raised eyebrows.

"That's *your* problem." Wynter's nostrils twitch like somebody passed gas. Her dark brown hair and eyebrows are tiger-streaked with platinum, and her eye shadow matches. Her boobs look like grapefruit halves poking out of her pink V-neck tee.

Tessa spreads her fingers to better admire her talons. "Bring her if you have to." I've always envied her olive skin and wavy blue-black hair, but no torture has been devised that would make me admit it.

Before I can say, "I'd rather stick my tongue in a food processer than talk to those two sluts," Laurel has my arm in a vise grip and is dragging me over. She thinks Tessa and Wynter stand at the pinnacle of the popularity pyramid. Manny tells me they're more familiar with the horizontal position.

Once we arrive at their magic tree house, I notice that the popularity princesses have made themselves a mat out of opened textbooks. Last year I spilled one drop of Pepsi on my algebra book and had to pay a two-dollar fine. Twenty bucks says they'll wiggle out of paying for all those broken spines.

They leave us standing while Tessa files her nails and Wynter adds another coat of lipstick. Just as I'm about to execute a quick turnaround and kick dirt in their faces, Tessa speaks.

"This is the situation, *Laurel*," she says, using an orange stick to push back her cuticles. "When you started school last fall, Wynter and I were somewhat interested. Your look isn't awful, and—since you're from Chicago—we thought you had more potential than the bumpkins who've lived here forever." Tessa flicks her eyes toward me.

"Unfortunately," Wynter takes up the narrative, "you disappointed us with your poor choice of friends."

Hmm. Who can they be talking about?

It's Tessa's turn again. "Until last week, when we read your post on Facebook . . ."

Am I the only person in school who didn't see Laurel's cyber Pig Proclamation?

". . . and we thought you were getting it together." Tessa sticks the tip of the orange stick in her mouth, which seems borderline gross to me. "Pigs in Hammond's office would have been too perfect."

Wynter adjusts her bra to give "the girls" more exposure. One more adjustment and their pink noses will be getting sunburned. "But, after all the hype, you disappointed us again. Although," she pauses for effect, "I heard that a trash can outside the teachers' lounge was crammed full of shredded toilet paper this morning. And one of the senior girls stepped in a gross pile of stuff in the elevator. Almost like something went on here last night." She locks eyes with Laurel. "Do you know anything about that?"

Laurel is so eager to please that she's practically wagging her tail. "Well, actually, we—"

"Heard that rumor too," I cut in, "but it doesn't have anything to do with pigs." I search for a plausible story. "This morning I overheard two of the custodians saying a bunch of sophomore girls sneaked in Saturday morning and TP'ed the teachers' lounge. The girls were on their way out of the building when Principal Hammond stopped them and asked what they were doing." I can't believe this total BS is coming out of my mouth. "Of course, one of them broke down and confessed, and they had to clean it all up." Laurel is gaping at me like I've sprouted another pair of arms.

Wynter leans back on her elbows and studies me from under her fake eyelashes. "You're saying nothing at all happened last night?"

"Not as far as I know." I hope my quivering stomach doesn't come up with a different story.

Wynter looks at Laurel again. "I don't know anything either," Laurel says glumly.

"So, instead of partying with us this summer, I guess you and Poplar"—Tessa twitches her upper lip at me— "will be sitting in her backyard watching the grass grow. Unless, of course, you find a way to convince us that you're ready to move up to the big leagues."

Laurel's eyes are bright. Her overeager expression reminds me of Carmine hoping for a treat. "Now that you bring it up, I'm sort of planning—"

"Her name's not Poplar," Wynter interrupts. "It's Un-Poplar. Which she totally is." She and Tessa laugh.

Without waiting for Laurel, I stomp over to the archery line. Getting my hands on a lethal weapon is looking like a good idea after all.

seven

FOR THE REST OF THE DAY, I'M PEEVED AT LAUREL BECAUSE she didn't stand up for me when Tessa and Wynter dissed me. I'm even more pissed off that she hung around talking with them for at least five minutes after I walked away. So after school I go home instead of hanging out at her place like I usually do.

With the stress of school behind me for today, mind-numbing fatigue sets in. As I open the front door—so, so softly—I can almost see the dotted blue lines along the floor and up the stairs to my room. All I have to do is follow the path to fourteen hours of absolutely essential sleep.

Not daring to breathe, I swing the door shut gently,

gently. It closes with a click so faint that radar couldn't pick it up.

Mom bursts out of the family room like a jack-in-the-box.

"Hello! I'm glad you're home." She waves a limp rag in greeting. In her other hand she's holding a spray bottle of all-surface cleaner. After we cleaned all weekend, what can possibly be dirty?

"Carmine has been scratching at the back door ever since I got home from work an hour ago. Your dad said he rolled in something and can't come in until you give him a bath. So hurry up before he scratches all the paint off the door."

Any other time I'd try to talk my way out of it, but lack of sleep has stupefied my brain. Mom won't leave me alone until I give Carmine his imaginary bath. "Okay. As soon as I change."

My foot is moving toward the bottom step when she says, "While you're walking Carmine, you'll need to drop by Miriam Simmons's house and give her an invitation to Manny's party."

Fear and loathing overcome my stupefaction. "Can't you just mail it?"

"No, I cannot 'just mail it,'" Mom says as she sprays and scrubs a microscopic speck on the wall. "I overlooked Miriam when I wrote the guest list, and sending an invitation at this late date would be inexcusably tacky."

"It's Manny's party. Why can't he take the invitation?"

Mom stops scrubbing to glare at me. "Manny is working at the golf course. And, even if he weren't, you'll be walking right past Miriam's house. I can't believe you're complaining about handing an invitation to a lonely old woman."

"I have to *hand* it to her?" I cover my eyes as Mom aims the spray bottle at me. "If it was anybody else, I wouldn't mind, but Miss Simmons hates me. Last week when I tried to carry her groceries, she attacked me with her walker."

Mom laughs. "Miriam Simmons wouldn't attack anyone. She's as meek as a kitten."

"More like a saber-toothed tiger," I mutter.

"I'm sure you'll be safe with Carmine to protect you." She cocks an ear toward the thumping back door. "If he isn't worn out from destroying our house."

Which returns us to the beginning of the discussion. "Fine. Whatever you say."

"I'm glad to hear that because, after you deliver the invitation, you have to clean your room. It looks—and smells—worse than a pigsty."

Upstairs, I have to concede that Mom is right. My room smells like a hog lot on a hot day. I stick my head into the hall, gulp air, and dash over to crank my windows open. When there's enough fresh air to let me breathe without gagging, I gather up last night's clothes, rip the sheets off my bed, and dump everything down the laundry chute in the hall.

Carmine does his crazy dog dance when he sees me at the gate. Several carefully placed hip and knee blocks get me into the yard. Now that I'm within smelling range, I know an imaginary bath isn't going to be enough. He has the same hog-lot smell as my bedroom, and the brownish crust on his back and paws isn't milk chocolate.

Giving Carmine a bath is never a problem. I drag the tub from the garage, and he jumps into it before I run the water. He likes the water, the shampoo, and even the conditioner. But his favorite part is after I've toweled him off. Then he runs in circles, shakes, and rolls on every inch of the yard—his version of the canine triathlon. I'm almost as wet as he is when he's finished, but I'm awake.

After I catch Carmine and put on his collar again, I assess my chances of swiping his leash from the hook inside the front door without being caught. When we get back from our walk I'll say I forgot about delivering the invitation. Mom won't believe me, but she might be so disgusted that she'll do it herself.

Carmine follows me around the house to the front door. I could probably walk him without a leash unless he saw a squirrel or a cat or another dog or . . . Yeah, I definitely need the leash.

I push his rump onto the front step. "Carmine, stay here. I'll be right back. Stay."

Opening the door the smallest amount possible, I slide

my hand through the crack and reach for the leash. Bare wall.

Okay, I'm not far enough. I slide my arm in up to the shoulder and feel around the wall. Ah, there it is.

Carefully, I lift it off the hook. Crap! It's caught on something. I jiggle it, but it's still stuck. What can it be caught on?

Forget it! I shove the door wide open and step inside.

"Are you looking for this?" Mom holds up her wrist with the handle of the leash wrapped around it. She puts it and an envelope into my hand. "Be sure to tell Miriam I said hello."

How can a woman who looks so normal be pure evil?

Carmine pulls me down the sidewalk in his sled dog imitation. Every few feet he drags me onto the grass so he can sniff and pee. Some woman on TV referred to it as "reading the pee mail." What's he checking on—dog food brands, filtered or unfiltered water, neutered or sexually active? Since Carmine stacks up in the neutered column, that would be depressing.

As we reach Miss Simmons's front porch, a dark cloud passes over the sun, and the birds stop singing. Carmine's ears droop. He plops his rump on the sidewalk, stares at the House of Doom, and whines.

"I hear you, buddy. I'll make this as quick as possible."

Miss Simmons's house is an old white two-story with a creaky front porch flanked on both sides by overgrown evergreen bushes. Cottonwoods and green ash trees shade the house and yard, and pink honeysuckle borders the cracked asphalt driveway. When I try to drag Carmine up the steps with me, he digs his toes into the sidewalk. I give up and hang his leash over the porch rail.

Miss Simmons's front door jerks open as I'm reaching for her doorbell. "What do you think you're doing?" she screeches. Her eyes blaze, her face is red, and she's hanging on to a walker tricked out with a Velcro cup holder, an umbrella holder, and a blue canvas magazine sleeve. Gutted tennis balls cushion the bottoms of the walker's two back legs. "Unhook that beast from my front porch before he rips out my railing!"

I look at my poor dog shivering on the sidewalk. To keep Miss Simmons from bonking me with her walker, I step down and move Carmine to a rusty fence post at the corner of what used to be a vegetable garden. I swear I can see gratitude in his eyes.

"Sorry," I tell her. I walk back up to the house and hold out Manny's invitation. "I just came to give you this."

Miss Simmons throws her hands in front of her face, and her walker swishes past my bare shins. "I'm not sub-scribing to any magazines or buying any cookies!"

Now she's pissing me off. I try to hand her an envelope,

and she acts like I'm the Cottonwood Creek Strangler. "It's just an invitation to—"

My tongue goes numb when a skunk waddles out from under the evergreen bushes on my left. I back against the wall and hold out my arm to keep Miss Simmons from stepping onto the porch. "Look out! That's a skunk!"

Carmine jumps to his feet and lets out a string of high-pitched barks. His leash snaps tight. Ignoring him, the skunk waddles to the bottom of the steps.

I try to run for cover, but my flip-flops skid like Wile E. Coyote on a bad day. "Quick! Let me in and close the door!"

Miss Simmons uses her walker to hold me off. "Would you quit blocking the door? And stop yelling. You're scaring Sammy Stripers."

I freeze as the skunk toddles up the steps and stops at my feet. Holding my breath—for more than one reason—I slide away from the door as it wanders into Miss Simmons's house.

"B-B-But, Miss Simmons. You just let a sk-skunk into your house."

She levels a stern look at me. "Nonsense. That's nothing but my old tomcat, Sammy."

The old bat's brain has flown out of its cave. "That was no tomcat; that was a skunk. You know, the wild animal that spreads rabies and distemper, not to mention the god-awful smell if it sprays you."

Miss Simmons marches out of her house and into my face. "Listen to me, young lady. What you just saw was an old tomcat." She sets a front wheel of her walker on my foot and puts enough pressure on it to get my attention. "And I'd better not hear that you've told anyone different. Do you understand me?"

Her face is deathly white, and her voice quivers underneath the tough talk. She's really worried someone will find out she's keeping a skunk for a pet. I used to wonder if Miss Simmons was crazy. Mystery solved.

"Seriously, I don't care how many skunks you have." I push her walker off my foot. "But I wouldn't want them sneaking into our house through Carmine's dog door."

"Don't get smart with me, miss, or I'll give you a thrashing." Miss Simmons shakes her walker so hard she has to hold on to the doorframe for support.

I imagine her chasing me around the yard, pushing her walker, and I have to bite my lips to keep from laughing. "Sorry," I finally manage. "Please just take this invitation to Manny's graduation party, and I'll go away."

Miss Simmons eyes the envelope and finally takes it from my hand. "When and where is this party?"

"Our house next Saturday, from one to five." Having done my duty—and nearly escaped with my life—I'm anxious to get away.

"Of course I'll have to check my calendar, but I can

probably come over for a little while," she says, as if she'd be doing us a favor.

"That's . . . good. Mom will be"—I wrack my brain for the right word—"thrilled."

I scamper down the steps and free Carmine. "Well, I guess we'll see you Saturday," I call over my shoulder.

"Wait," she says. I stop, and Carmine nearly jerks my shoulder from the socket. "Tell Manfred not to expect a gift from me. I believe a graduation card will be sufficient."

"Okay," I choke out. "I'll be sure to tell him that."

eight

SENIORS HAVE THEIR LAST CLASSES ON THURSDAY, MAY 19.
On Friday, school dismisses early so families can prepare
for the graduation ceremony at seven that night. Since
the weather is clear, Cottonwood Creek holds graduation in the football stadium with seniors' families and
friends sitting in the bleachers. Laurel and I sit in the row
behind Mom and Dad and watch Manny and the other
105 members of his class get their diplomas. I get a little
misty-eyed when it sinks in that Manny will be gone in
three months, and I'll be able to store my extra stuff in
his closet.

Mom has Dad and me up until almost midnight Friday
putting the "finishing touches" on the house for the party

on Saturday. Naturally, Manny is absent. Mr. Mattheson, the golf/track/softball coach and history/driver's ed teacher, is holding an after-graduation open house for all his players/students. When Manny told Mom Friday morning that he felt obligated to go, I choked on the little marshmallow hearts in my cereal. I don't know one person at Cottonwood Creek High who feels obligated to do anything Mr. Matt says. He's such a personality powerhouse that his coaching stories put student drivers to sleep behind the wheel. But Manny laid the "senior year" card on the table, and Mom believed him for the thousand-and-first time.

Wait until next year, when I pull out the list I'm keeping of all the crap Manny's getting away with because he's a senior. If Mom needs help putting my senior party together, she'd better adopt Martha Stewart. I'll be unavailable from April through June.

At three a.m. I wake to the peaceful rhythm of Manny puking his guts out in the bathroom across the hall. Before I pull the pillow over my ears, I set my alarm for nine o'clock. I've decided to prepare something extra special for his breakfast.

When Manny still hasn't shown his face by nine thirty Saturday morning, I unlatch his door and send Carmine in to make a wake-up call. Soon I hear the thump of

Carmine's sixty pounds landing in the middle of Manny's stomach.

This is followed by a series of gagging sounds and curses. "Carmine, you hairy turd! Get off me!" Although I hate to break up the happy reunion between a boy and his dog, I call Carmine off before Manny wakes up enough to do him any damage.

When I peek inside his room, Manny is sitting up in bed with the sheets tangled around his waist. His face is the color of wet cement, and his eyes are puffy. "What the hell are you doing, trying to kill me?"

The thought has crossed my mind.

"No, I'm trying to keep you from hurting Mom's feelings. Even though she's been up since dawn getting ready for your party—the one you haven't helped with one bit," I say, slapping down the whole deck of guilt cards, "she's in the kitchen putting together a cheese omelet especially for you. So get your butt downstairs before it gets cold, or she'll see what a selfish, ungrateful brat you really are."

While Manny's—hopefully—writhing with guilt, I dash to the kitchen, switch on a burner, and dump in the eggs I've scrambled to a perfect froth. The preparation of this omelet must be carefully timed. As long as Manny does his usual ten-minute bathroom search for new whiskers and Mom stays outdoors ordering Dad around, I'm golden.

Speaking of golden, the smell of frying eggs is making my stomach growl. Too bad there were only three eggs left after Mom and I made a mountain of deviled eggs for the party.

I carefully lift the edges of the omelet with a spatula and let the raw egg run underneath. When it's thick and puffy, I expertly flip it over to let the other side brown. Now comes the tricky part. From a bowl I've set aside, I pour in my secret ingredients: a quarter cup of crushed Tums lovingly blended into a half cup of a Pepto Bismol/Tabasco sauce mixture. If this doesn't cure Manny's hangover, nothing will.

As I'm folding the omelet and pressing the edges together, the toilet flushes overhead. What timing! I lay three slices of cheddar cheese across the top and stand back to admire my masterpiece. Then I pull out my cell phone and snap a picture. I leave the phone in easy reach for more pictures to come.

I've just removed the pan from the burner when Manny walks in. His hair and face are wet, but he still looks like the mummy unwrapped. By the way his mouth is puckered, I can see he's one gag reflex away from puking.

"God, Manny! What outhouse did you fall into last night? You look like a pile of crap!"

Manny pulls out a chair and falls into it. "Not so loud," he groans. "My head hurts from the waist up." He leans over the table and massages his eyes with the heels of his hands.

I set a glass of grapefruit juice in front of him. "Wait till I tell Mom and Dad that Mr. Mattheson throws drinking parties for the senior class. Mom's head will do a complete three-sixty."

"Don't even joke about it. I spent ten minutes at Mr. Matt's house last night, and it felt like a decade." Manny takes a sip of juice and cringes. "I need to eat something solid before my stomach comes out through my nose."

There's my cue. I slide the omelet from the pan onto his plate. Even though I know what's inside, it looks so delicious that my mouth waters.

"So what was that story you told Mom about 'feeling obligated' to attend the senior party?" I indulge my rising anger and grip the handle of the skillet more firmly. I can't bash in Manny's head, but fantasizing about it makes me feel better.

"Man, that smells great," Manny says. "Where's Mom, anyway?"

"Dad's setting up the 'in case of rain' tent. She's supervising." Anticipation is making my palms sweat.

"Poor Dad." Manny pokes the edge of the omelet with his fork.

Eat it already!

"Yeah. She's had both of us working like dogs. So where were you last night?"

"A party at some farmhouse. At least half the senior class was there." He cuts off a small piece, forks it into his mouth, and chews. "This tastes great! Just what the doctor ordered."

You don't know the half of it.

"So how come you're not eating?" he asks.

"Mom, Dad, and I ate together hours ago," I lie. "Mom wanted to let you sleep so you'd be rested for your party."

"She's the best." Manny takes another bite. He has this weird habit of eating all the edges before he cuts into the center. All the more for him to hurl. "I need to do something nice for her, maybe a belated Mother's Day card."

"I don't think Hallmark has come up with those yet."

The back door opens and Dad heads straight to the coffee pot. The remains of his hair look like a helicopter landing zone. He fills his #1 DAD mug to the brim and gulps. "Ah! The fluid of life!"

I channel my mental powers into sending Dad back outdoors. "What smells so good?" He zeros in on Manny's omelet. "Hey, where did that come from?"

"Mom made it for him—with the last three eggs."

Dad thinks that over, probably trying to figure out when Mom quit nagging him long enough to throw an omelet together. Then he shrugs and pulls out the chair beside Manny. "How about splitting your breakfast with the old man?"

Manny shovels another bite into his mouth. "Aspen said you guys already ate."

Dad cocks his head at me, no doubt wondering about the breakfast we didn't eat together. Since I don't know the signal for, "I'm playing a practical joke on Manny so don't mess me up," I just nod and smile.

"So what?" Dad finally says. "It won't kill you to spare a few bites, seeing as how I've been busting my hump getting things ready for you."

"Okay," Manny says with a pained sigh. "After I take a couple more bites you can have the rest." He digs his fork into the center of the omelet, chops off about half of it, and crams the huge chunk into his mouth.

How could I have doubted my brother's greed?

As Manny begins to chew, my fingers tiptoe across the table to my cell phone. My first snap captures the moment when his eyes bug at the first hit of Pepto and Tabasco. And there's the stomach-clutching and gagging that might or might not have come from the minty taste of Tums. Of course, I don't miss the "I'll kill you" glare in his eyes just before he dashes to the downstairs bathroom. I consider trying for a bathroom shot, but that might be taking it too far.

Dad laces his fingers across his stomach and studies Manny's half-empty plate. "So I probably shouldn't eat the rest of that omelet?"

"I wouldn't recommend it."

He shakes his head. "That's too bad. I was really hungry for one."

"I'll make you one next Saturday."

"Same ingredients?" he asks.

"Not exactly."

"Glad to hear it." Dad goes to the coffeepot and refills his mug. "You'll clean up the kitchen before your mother comes in?"

"Spic and span."

"That's one of the reasons you're my favorite daughter."

"And you're my favorite dad."

We both stop to listen to Manny retching in the bathroom.

Dad nods in that direction. "Senior parties are rough on the stomach. Might have to clean that up, too."

I smile. "That's okay."

Dad smiles back. "Well, once more into the breach." With a resigned sigh, he closes the door behind him.

As I dump the remains of Manny's omelet into the disposal, I catch myself humming.

The afternoon weather is nauseatingly perfect—blue sky, gentle breeze, birds singing in three-part harmony. Any minute I'm expecting a carload of A-list celebrities to cruise by and decide to stop in for refreshments. That's the kind of luck Manny has.

Speaking of which, he looks way too good for a guy who was blowing his intestines into the john three hours ago. Just before the party, he corners me in the upstairs hall. "That omelet was kick-ass. It knocked the alcohol out of my system in three minutes flat," he says. "I've never felt this good after a night of drinking."

"Naturally. It's the number-one hangover cure on the Internet," I bluff, keeping my arms crossed over my midsection. Experience has taught me never to leave my diaphragm unprotected. "I knew you'd want to feel good for your graduation party."

"Is that so?" Manny straightens the collar of his favorite golf shirt. "I didn't realize you were looking out for my health, Sis. Then it's only fair for me to do something for you, too." The creepy serial killer cadence of his voice makes my earlobes prickle. "I'm going to make sure you get lots and lots of healthful exercise by keeping you out of my car. For the entire summer."

I have to cover my mouth to keep from spitting on the back of his neck as he saunters away.

nine

I'M LURKING ON A FOLDING CHAIR IN THE CORNER OF THE totally unnecessary tent Dad spent two hours setting up and wishing Laurel would hurry up and get here. Our house and lawn are swarming with aunts, uncles, cousins, and grandparents. I've wiped enough old-lady lipstick off my cheek to paint a mural. On the plus side, finals are over, Manny's graduation ceremony wasn't as torturous as I thought it would be, and I'm a free woman for the next eleven weeks.

Golden boy Manny is working the crowd, spreading rays of sunshine to one and all. His party has barely started, but he's doled out enough hugs, kisses, and handshakes to be elected president. I'd be cheery, too, if an overflowing basket of graduation cards filled with money was waiting for me at the end of the day. But I notice Manny is doing frequent visual sweeps of our yard so he doesn't miss the arrival of any of the dozens of girls he invited. I wonder how Cynthia likes sharing him with all those female friends.

"Aspen, there you are! I've been looking everywhere." Mom's face is damp with sweat, and the peach-colored dress she bought especially for today is already wilting. "I need your help in the kitchen."

I should have waited for Laurel behind the garage. "You look stressed, Mom. Is everything okay?"

"Your Aunt Sharon is driving me to the brink of insanity!" Mom dabs her forehead with a napkin. "Count your lucky stars that you have a brother instead of a sister."

"I was just offering up a prayer of gratitude."

But Mom is too frazzled to appreciate my wit. "If I hear one more time about how gifted her precious Jeremy is, I'll pull her tongue out by the roots."

And I thought that side of Mom's personality was saved for me.

"And if that weren't enough—" Her sentence ends in a yelp. "My stars! Why are the police here?"

Mom grabs my wrist and jerks. My left foot catches on the brace of the folding chair. It collapses around my ankle and sends me reeling into Mom. I snatch at the edge of the closest table for support, but it tips on the uneven lawn. And just that fast, Mom and I are sprawled on the grass, with lawn furniture piled on top of us.

I lie there, listening to my heartbeat, wriggling my fingers and toes to make sure they're still working. My head is on Mom's shoulder, and I hear her breathing. I wonder if she and I are thinking the same thing—it wouldn't be so bad to hang out under here until this party thing blows over.

Before I have a chance to ask if we should have Dad throw a tablecloth over us, the table is tipped aside and someone pulls the chair off my ankle. I keep my eyes closed in accordance with the law of "If I Can't See You, You Can't See Me."

"Miss, are you all right?" an unfamiliar voice asks. "Will I hurt you if I help you stand up?"

Only my self-esteem.

"I'm okay," I mumble, "but I think I squashed my mother." When two pairs of hands take my upper arms, I have no choice but to open my eyes. Holding my left arm is a short, black-haired cop with a thickset torso and a mustache. Holding my left arm is—

Oh, crap!

"Aspen, are you sure you're okay?" Clay asks, his blue eyes narrowed with concern. "That looked like a nasty fall."

Beside me, Dad and the cop are helping Mom up. She's a little wobbly, but she says she's all right.

"Excellent! That's exactly what Mom and I were going for." I reach up and smooth my hair. "The party was dragging, so we thought we'd throw in a little excitement."

Clay smiles and squeezes my arm, which he's still holding. "It's great the way you take everything in stride. My mom's like that, too."

Goody. There's nothing like having a cute guy compare me to his mother.

Dad rests his hand on my shoulder. "Aspen, honey, are you hurt?" When I tell him I'm in one piece, he says, "That's my girl." He nods at the cop standing beside him. "This is Miguel Sierra, the newest addition to Cottonwood Creek's police force."

"Nice to meet you, Aspen," Officer Sierra says, shaking my hand. "For a moment I thought I'd have to call on my CPR training. I'm glad it didn't come to that."

"Me, too," I say, distracted because Clay has let go of my arm.

Officer Sierra smiles, showing two rows of white teeth. "When I saw the crowd, I decided to stop and introduce myself."

"That's a relief." Mom brushes some grass trimmings out of her hair. "I thought we were being raided."

Officer Sierra sees my uncle and grandparents, who

are hurrying over to find out what's wrong. "Well, you might keep an eye on that bunch. They look like they could get rowdy." He holds out his hand to Clay. "You must be Aspen's brother."

"No!" I say too loudly. "This is my brother's friend, Clay . . ." I realize I don't know his last name.

"Clay Mason. I have a farm just north of town."

"I don't know the area all that well yet," Officer Sierra says. "Do you live out on Whitetail Road?"

"Aspen," Mom hisses in my ear, "go tell everyone why Officer Sierra is here before any rumors get started."

I'm trying to hear what Clay is saying. "But—"

"Now!" She gives me a shove that's not exactly gentle.

I stalk off to do her bidding. It would serve her right if I told Aunt Sharon that Mom's being arrested for prostitution.

While I spread the word among my relatives that we're not being hauled off to the slammer, I keep an eye on Clay. After helping Dad set up the table, he wanders over to where Manny is treating a group of girls to his charm and half-wit. Manny's girlfriend, Cynthia, however, is not among the lucky few. I wonder what that's about.

Why am I worrying about Cynthia? Clay has stumbled into an all-you-can-eat buffet of horny girls, and my traitorous brother is introducing him to all of them. Okay, so I haven't told Manny I'm interested in Clay. A good brother would know. Tessa and Wynter slink up to their little group, and my blood heads for the boiling point. Why did Manny have to invite those two man-eaters?

"Aspen, there's a cop car parked in front of your house!" Laurel shrieks, tackling me from behind. "Did they find out?"

"Relax." I push Laurel off without registering what she's saying. My whole being is focused on Wynter, who's rubbing her elevated boobs on Clay's arm. He looks around as if he's not sure what to do. I close my eyes, channeling all of my mental energy toward him.

Wynter repels you. You want Aspen. Wynter repels you. You want Aspen.

When I open my eyes, Wynter has her hand on the back of Clay's neck while she whispers in his ear. I am *this close* to losing faith in my psychic abilities.

Laurel shakes me like a rag doll. "Aspen, stop daydreaming and listen! Some cop has your father cornered by the back door. I think he's being interrogated!"

I look over her shoulder. "No, he's not. Everything's fine." Except that from here, it looks like the school slut is polishing Clay's right ear with her tongue.

"What is wrong with you?" Laurel grabs both sides of my head and pulls me down to her eye level. Neck strain is one disadvantage of having a best friend who's six inches shorter than I am. "What will our parents do if we get busted for the pig thing?"

"Excuse me, Aspen." Officer Sierra materializes at my elbow. "I'm leaving now. Still feeling okay?"

Laurel's eyes swell like hard-boiled eggs, and her body jerks like she's been tasered.

"I-I'm fine, Officer Sierra. Th-Thanks for asking." My heart hits three beats in quick succession and stops dead. How much of Laurel's rant did he hear?

"Good deal." There's no time to channel my mental energy before he asks, "And who's your friend?"

"Laura Mae Hamsenburger," Laurel blurts. "From Australia. I'm visiting for the weekend."

Officer Sierra strokes his mustache. "You traveled all the way from Australia just to spend the weekend?"

"She's such a kidder!" I throw my arm around Laurel's neck and pull her against my side. "This is my friend Laurel Piedmont. And she lives in Cottonwood Creek—not Australia."

"Well, Laurel, you've got quite a sense of humor," Officer Sierra says, but I'd feel better if he was smiling. "So did I hear you say something about a pig?"

Laurel's mouth drops open.

Think, think, think!

"A pig?" I say as innocently as my pounding heart will allow. "Oh, Laurel, Officer Sierra must have heard what you said about the hog confinement."

Please, Laurel, just play along!

"Oh, that." She sounds like a robot with a low battery. With my arm still around her neck, I drag her into a huddle with Cottonwood Creek's finest. "See, Officer Sierra, we've heard that the city council might allow a hog confinement west of town." I lower my voice. "We want to protest against it at the next town council meeting, but Laurel's worried that staging a protest might be against a city ordinance or something."

Officer Sierra raises the brim on his hat—the better to see our lying eyes. "Is that so?" TV cops use that same tone just before they drag guilty suspects off to prison.

"I told her we wouldn't—you know, get into trouble—because it's a free country and all, but . . ." Why doesn't he pull out his baton and knock me unconscious so I'll stop babbling? "So would we get arrested for protesting?"

His cop stare shifts from Laurel to me and back again. "That depends. If you march outside carrying signs, no problem. But if you physically or verbally disrupt the council meeting, you might be in trouble."

"See, Laurel, I told you we could," I gush, bobbing my head like I'm demented. "Well, thanks for the info, Officer Sierra. It was really nice to meet you," I add, trying to simultaneously suck up and usher him out.

"Yeah, really nice," Laurel adds in her low-battery robot voice. If I choose a life of crime, she'll make a lousy alibi witness.

But Officer Sierra is not a man who takes a hint. He spreads his feet and settles in like he plans to spend the afternoon. "See, girls, the word *pig* caught my attention because a farmer northwest of town, name of Dale Crawford, had some trouble with his pigs a week or so ago. On a Sunday night, I believe it was."

Laurel gulps.

"Oh?" I say, because he seems to be waiting for one of us to say something. "What happened?" Itchy sweat is trickling into my butt crack.

"Well, Dale's not quite sure. His dogs started making a commotion about ten thirty or thereabouts, which isn't unusual with all the critters stirring at night. But after an hour of them carrying on, he got up and checked. He said everything seemed fine." Officer Sierra runs a finger under his collar. "Around three in the morning the dogs started up again. Since there wasn't anything amiss the first time, he let it go."

"Hmm." I really, really want to scratch my butt crack.

"But in the morning he found tire tracks by the hog lot."

"Really?" I release my chokehold on Laurel in case we have to make a run for it.

"Here's the funny part," Officer Sierra says. "One of his gilts had popcorn around her snout."

It's my turn to gulp. "Popcorn?" I squeak like Mickey Mouse on helium.

"Popcorn." His hat shadows his eyes, but I feel them drilling into my brain. "That got him to checking his other pigs, and guess what?"

Laurel and I shake our heads in unison.

"He found popcorn on two of his other gilts."

My vocal cords are paralyzed.

A manic light comes on in Laurel's eyes. "Well, maybe they went to a movie. You know, sort of a 'gilts night out'?" She starts to giggle. "I think *Babe* is playing at the Newton drive-in theater."

I clench my teeth against a laugh, but it escapes as a snort.

Officer Sierra shakes his head. "You are a funny one," he says to Laurel. "Well, Dale said there was no harm done." He touches the brim of his hat. "You young ladies have a nice day."

"You too, Officer Sierra," we chorus.

As soon as the police car pulls out of sight, Laurel collapses against me. "Do you think he knows?"

I unstick my underwear from my butt crack. "He thinks he knows something but he doesn't know what it is. And as long as he doesn't know, he can't accuse us of anything."

Laurel nods. "You know, you're right. If we both stay strong, we'll be fine."

My knees fold under me, and for the second time today,

I'm sprawled on the ground. So much for staying strong.

"Aspen, are you all right?" Clay appears at my side.

Why is Fate out to get me? "I'm fine," I say, pushing myself up to a sitting position. "I just got dizzy for a second."

"Are you sure you didn't hit your head earlier?" I shake my head again and try to stand. Clay takes my hands and pulls me up. Then he puts his arm around my waist and leads me to a chair. "Laurel, stay with her while I get some water." He dashes toward the coolers by the house.

"Are you sick or something?" Laurel asks.

"No, I think I'm just dehydrated. Of course, the blind terror didn't help either." I straighten my rumpled top and check it for grass stains. "When Clay comes back, could you maybe go talk to someone else for a little bit?"

"I could make that sacrifice." Laurel pulls a lip gloss from the pocket of her white denim shorts and adjusts her red V-neck tank top. Her earrings are vertical chains of three gold hearts, and a tiny diamond sparkles from the heart-shaped gold locket dangling in her cleavage. If I had cleavage like hers, my locket would be in the shape of an arrow pointing at it. "I read on Facebook that Manny broke up with Cynthia Burson last night. If I'm lucky, he's taking applications for a summer rebound girl." She hikes up her boobs and tugs her shorts lower on her hips. "Good luck to both of us."

As soon as Laurel sees Clay returning, she saunters off.

The way she's swinging her hips, her shorts may be around her ankles before she reaches Manny. Which should get his attention—at least temporarily.

Clay hands me a bottle of water, which I chug like a wino after a weekend in the drunk tank. "Yeah, you were thirsty," he says when I set the empty bottle on the table. "You look better now that your face is pink instead of white."

"Thanks." I wipe my mouth with the back of my hand. "How did you get here so fast? A minute ago, Wynter was whispering in your ear."

Clay grins. "Does that mean you were watching me?"

"No, uh, well . . ." My face is scalding. "It's just . . . not many guys would leave her to—"

He glances over at Wynter, who's cuddling up to a stocky football player–type I don't recognize. Poor Laurel is trying to wade through the sea of girls around Manny. I hope she doesn't get trampled. "Wynter has some visible assets, but she's too aggressive for my taste." Clay shrugs. "Besides, I couldn't pass up the chance to rescue you twice in the same day."

I wish I had a bag of ice to dump into my bra. "I'm not always so high maintenance. You've been lucky enough to catch me at my worst."

When Clay smiles, little lines fan out from the corners of his eyes. I wonder how many years ago he graduated.

I'm turning seventeen next month, so as long as he's not outrageously ancient—like older than twenty-one—Mom and Dad won't freak too much.

He pulls out a chair and straddles it backward. The sun brings out his freckles and sparks the red highlights in his hair. "I wouldn't say that. The first time I saw you, you were wrangling pigs. Nothing catches a farm boy's attention like a girl who knows her way around livestock."

As much as I'd like to hear about Clay being interested in me, his pig comment takes me back to the conversation Laurel and I just had with our new law enforcement friend. "Did Officer Sierra ask you any questions?"

Clay looks puzzled at the sudden change of topic. "Not really. Why?"

"He heard Laurel say the word *pig* and asked us a bunch of questions about that Crawford guy's pigs."

Clay rests his arms on the back of the chair. "So what did you say?"

Is Clay thinking we ratted him out? "Don't worry. We acted like we didn't know anything about them."

He frowns. "Why? You didn't do anything wrong."

"Try telling that to my parents," I say. "I don't think they'd be convinced."

His frown deepens. "I'd guess Officer Sierra wasn't convinced either."

My stomach twists like a pretzel. "Why not?"

"Because he already knew the whole story."

My stomach pretzel twists tighter. "You mean the *whole*, whole story?"

"I imagine so. Tuesday night I called Dale and told him what happened." Clay shifts his weight on the chair. "If I hadn't had a seed convention in Waterloo on Monday, I'd have called him sooner."

"You told him . . ." I'm too overcome with panic to finish the sentence.

"A farmer's livestock is his livelihood, Aspen." Clay sounds more like a parent than a potential boyfriend. "If one of those gilts turned up sick, Dale needed to know what to tell the vet." He brushes his hair out of his eyes. "The only thing I couldn't tell him was who took his pigs in the first place."

My mind can't process this much disastrous news at once. Okay, Laurel and I didn't lie to Officer Sierra—technically—but playing dumb was almost as bad.

Clay is waiting for me to name the guilty parties, but I value my life too much to rat out Buttferk. Laurel and I haven't forgotten Ferret's threatening Facebook message or Buttferk cornering us outside the school building. Laurel's place has a home alarm system, but my family's only alarm system is Carmine, and he'd rat me out to Jack the Ripper for a hamburger. Buttferk hasn't taken revenge yet, but the thought of them skulking through our house with knives freezes my blood. "Whoever did it was gone by the time we got there." Aspen Parks tells another lie by omission.

"I see." Clay stares down at the grass.

I can almost read the questions playing through his mind, and I'm waiting for him to ask one of them. It might be worth being killed to wipe the disappointed look off his face.

"Aspen Parks, there you are! Come here this minute!" Miss Simmons bellows at me from half a block away. Her face is hidden under a dinner-plate-size sunhat, and she's pushing her walker at warp speed. "Hurry up!"

I want to clear things up with Clay, but I don't know what to say. Besides, he's already on his feet. "It looks like you're needed," he says. "Anyway, I have to take off."

A lump the size of a grapefruit is lodged in my throat. "Clay, I'm—"

"Right now, young lady!" Miss Simmons is louder than the town fire siren that goes off at noon every weekday.

"Bye, Aspen. Have a good summer." Which is guy talk for *I never want to see you again.*

I don't even get to watch Clay walk out of my life because Miss Simmons's screeching is drawing stares from my grandparents. I walk out to meet her.

"Is there a problem, Miss Simmons?"

"Of course there's a problem!" she snaps. "I could fall and break my neck on your unkempt lawn." She thrusts an empty Tupperware container into my hand. "I promised Sammy I'd bring him a snack. No sweets, mind you, just raw fruits and vegetables. But not broccoli. It gives him gas. And I won't tolerate that awful smell in my house!"

I'm too depressed to give that comment the comeback it deserves.

"Yes, Miss Simmons." With a sigh that reaches the soles of my feet, I lead her to the refreshment table.

If my future holds a worse day than today, let me die now.

ten

"WELCOME TO SUB STOP. HOW MAY I PLEASE YOUR TASTE BUDS today?" I drone into my headset. Only five days into this job, and I'm already saying the stupid words in my sleep. After I punch the order for two Barn Burner specials, an Iron Horse combo, and three jumbo root beer Washouts into the computer, I push back my red-striped conductor's hat and scratch my sweaty scalp. In between customers I look longingly at the sunshine—and gulp some air that isn't tainted with exhaust fumes—through the open drive-through window.

How could I have forgotten how mindlessly dreary this job is? It must be like what Mom says about child-birth—after it's over you forget the pain and focus on the end result. In my case, that's the whopping eight dollars an hour I'm raking in.

I wish I could forget the pain of Manny's graduation party, but every time I close my eyes I see Clay walking out of my life. After he left I found a chair for Miss Simmons near the buffet table and put Sammy's take-out meal in the container she brought. By the time I'd finished with that, Miss Simmons was holding Aunt Sharon by the wrist and treating her to a detailed description of her hip replacement surgery. Mom saw her sister in Miss Simmons's clutches, caught my eye, and beamed. I used the opportunity to escape to a table on the opposite side of our lawn.

A few minutes later Laurel found me. Her hair was a mess, she was limping, and there was a red punch stain on her white shorts. "What happened to you?" I asked.

Laurel collapsed into a chair and crossed her left foot over her knee. "I couldn't even get close enough to Manny to say hi." She showed me her swollen left big toe. "One of those sex-crazed freaks crushed my toe with her spiked heel. Who wears heels to a yard party?"

"Who spilled punch on your shorts?"

"Who knows? I was just glad to escape in one piece." Laurel tried to smooth down her hair, but it was a losing battle. "How did things go with Clay?"

I felt a sob building in my throat. "I'll tell you later—in private."

"That bad, huh?" Laurel patted my shoulder. "Look on the bright side. We'll be dateless together." She paused. "Except you'll have a job to keep you busy during the day, and I won't. What am I going to do while you're at work?"

I didn't have an answer for her. All I could think of was that last awful conversation with Clay.

In the two weeks since the party, I haven't heard from Clay. Not that he had any reason to call me. But at least there was hope before he discovered I tell lies to the police. In comparison, Wynter probably seems like a saint.

To make myself more miserable, I've been worming information about Clay from Manny one piece at time—without letting on that my interest is more than casual. I hope.

Through careful questioning, I've learned that Clay graduated two years ago from Waukee High. His parents retired from farming and moved to a condo in Altoona, leaving him to run the farm. He's taking agriculture classes at Iowa State in Ames, and he works part-time maintaining the golf course to help pay his tuition.

And he's not dating anyone. Which should make me feel better but doesn't. It's the second of June, the month of romance, and my only source of excitement is leaning against the vibrating smoothie machine.

"Hey, Parks, can you take another shift tonight?"

Willie Johnson, the Sub Stop manager, barks in my ear.

Startled, I stumble against the cash register. "I guess." Since the only engagement on my social calendar is my school physical in August, I might as well earn some money.

"Can't Christy make it?" I add. Christy Lawrence and I worked together all last summer. All that togetherness should have made us friends. Too bad she has the personality of a sour cherry.

"Christy bombed out on me." Willie fiddles with the red suspenders holding up the navy-striped denim pants that are part of his railroad engineer's outfit. Willie's half a foot taller than me, with thick brown hair that he combs every ten minutes. I'd guess he's in his late thirties, if I cared enough to guess.

"What do you mean?" I ask, trying not to sound too excited.

"At the last minute her parents decided to rent a cabin at Lake Okoboji for the summer," he growls. "Christy called me last night. Last night! How am I supposed to find someone to take her place at this short notice?"

A man pulls up to the menu board, and I take his order. "I might know someone," I say as soon as I'm finished.

"Really?" Willie hitches his pants over his skinny rear. "It better not be your boyfriend. That never works out."

As if I would have any way of knowing. "No, it's my friend Laurel Piedmont. She'll be a senior next year too, and she's really serious about wanting a summer job."

"Your friend, huh?" He rocks back on his heels. "Is she reliable?"

"Very," I say, crossing my fingers behind my back. All the fun Laurel and I will have working together overrides the history reports she's lost and the times she's been tardy to first period . . . and second period . . . and . . .

A mixture of hope and relief gleams in Willie's eyes. "Could she come in for an interview this afternoon?"

Even if I have to carry her piggyback. "Of course."

"Tell her to be here at two o'clock."

I call Laurel as soon as Willie wanders over to the bread ovens. The fourth time her cell goes over to voice mail, I switch to her landline.

"Whaaa?" She sounds like she's swimming in the bottom of a well.

"You're still asleep? It's after noon!"

"It's summer." She slurs the words into one. "Besides, there's nothing to get up for."

"There is now!" I tell Laurel the wonderful news. After I confirm—five times—that the interview is for real, I hold my cell at arm's length while she screams. When she's finished celebrating, I remind her that the job isn't a lock yet.

"Wear something casual but not too sexy," I caution her, "just in case Willie's wife is here. For reasons beyond my comprehension, she thinks every female she sees is hot for him."

"Casual but not sexy. Check." Laurel sounds wide awake now. Ear-splitting screams will do that for a person. "Anything else I need to know?"

Hmm. What else can I tell her about Willie's personality? To begin with, there's not much of it. "Answer Willie's questions as briefly as possible. And don't joke around. His sense of humor is nonexistent."

A pause. "Remind me again why I want to work there."

"Because of me, of course." Laurel better not back out on me. "Besides, once you pass the interview, Willie will be a non-issue. He spends most of his time in the storage room, browsing porn sites on the store's computer."

"Are you serious?" she gasps.

I laugh to myself at having shocked Laurel for a change. "Yes, about Willie being on the computer. As for the rest— I'm ninety-eight percent sure he's been neutered. I refuse to think beyond that."

"Good idea. I'm all about pure thoughts."

This time I laugh out loud. "Right. And I'm all about double-D bras."

The beeper on my headset goes off, and I look at the fuzzy computer screen to see who's waiting to order. Willie had a camera installed last summer after some smart-ass stuck a dozen adhesive-backed maxi pads on the menu board, and several customers complained. I would have helped myself, except they weren't the kind with wings.

Now there's just a frazzled-looking woman with a carload of hyperactive children. "Gotta go, Laurel. See you at two."

"Absolutely," she chirps. "I'll be there as soon as I find my bikini top and matching thong."

"Very funny!" I say as I close my phone. Laurel had better be kidding.

"Welcome to the Sub Stop. How may I please your taste buds today?" Laurel punches in the order and shuts off her headset. "Does Willie Wonka actually expect us to say that with a straight face?"

"Shut up! He's going to hear you." I set a cardboard tray of drinks on the ledge beside her and pray that Willie isn't behind us. He's standing about three strides away stacking bags of cucumber slices in the cooler. If it weren't for a rowdy bunch of middle school boys at the front counter, Laurel would be trying to pull her foot out of her mouth in front of our boss.

She's only been working here for three days—she started the morning after her interview—and she's already grousing. "You know you have to say that," I say for the tenth time. "It's on the first page of the employee manual."

Laurel hands the drinks out the window, and in the process flashes two inches of butt cleavage at the indoor population. A middle school boy waiting for his order tries to vault over the counter. I block his view of Laurel's rear and yank down her red conductor's vest.

She looks over her shoulder at me and shrugs. "Haven't read it. Don't plan to. If I need to know, you'll tell me."

"It's time to switch jobs anyway. I'll take the orders; you deliver." I press my fingers into my temples. "And watch where your butt's facing when you bend over." The guy working the counter hands the middle school kids their food. After one last, lustful gawk at Laurel's rear, they elbow and snicker their way out the door.

I've barely settled the headphones over my ears when a familiar male voice comes through. "I've heard the Sub Stop has the best food and the prettiest girls in town. Any truth to that?" When I look at the screen I see a grinning middle-aged man with his sunglasses pushed up on his forehead.

"Hi, Mr. Piedmont. How's it going?" Laurel's dad dresses up more than most men in Cottonwood Creek— probably because of his bank job—but he's super-nice. "I mean, how may I please your taste buds today?"

After Mr. Piedmont orders an Iron Horse special, he says, "I'm doing great, Aspen. Thank you again for helping Laurel land this job. Is she staying in line?"

"You know Laurel." Although I'm not so sure he really does. I wouldn't say Laurel puts on an act around her dad, but she definitely tones down her wild side. "She likes to keep things interesting."

Before her dad's car pulls up to the window, Laurel straightens her vest and hikes her shorts up to her waist. "Hi, Daddy. What are you doing here?"

Mr. Piedmont hands her a ten-dollar bill. "I'm heading to a meeting in Dallas Center, so I thought I'd grab a bite to eat on the road." He's a couple of inches taller than I am, probably five-ten, with brown hair, a roundish nose, and a ruddy face. His eyes are the same green as Laurel's, and he's smiling whenever I see him. "This is my only meeting today, so I should be home on time for a change. How about having popcorn-and-movie night?"

"That sounds good," Laurel says as she passes her dad his order. "I chose the movie last time, so it's your turn."

"At last! We've seen every Broadway musical at least three times." Mr. Piedmont rubs imaginary sweat off his forehead. "Tonight it's nothing but blood, guts, and glory."

Laurel makes a face. "Just so no animals get killed. You know I hate that."

"How could I forget?" Laurel's dad glances at his watch. "I'd better get going. Can't keep the clients waiting." He settles his sunglasses on his nose. "See you tonight, sweets.

Nice to see you again, Aspen. You'll have to come over for dinner sometime soon."

Laurel and I watch as Mr. Piedmont's car pulls out of the Sub Stop driveway and merges into traffic. "You have such a great dad," I tell her.

She tugs the top of her shorts below her navel again. "He's getting there. It won't be long before I have him completely trained."

For the next hour or so we can relax during the afternoon lull between the late lunchers and the early dinner crowd. Willie disappears into the storage room, and all the workers make themselves triple-decker subs and steal drinks from the soda fountain.

I settle onto the wooden stool inside the order window and take a brain-freezing slurp of my chocolate shake, or Massive Mudslide in Sub Stop terminology. Laurel drags a stool from the back and sits beside me. She's on her third refill of diet soda, even though the last thing she needs is a caffeine high. "Okay, so we've accomplished our first step, which is getting summer jobs. When our paychecks roll in, we move to step two: shopping for super-hot clothes. That gets us ready for step three: hitting the party circuit."

"I hate to burst your fantasy bubble, but Cottonwood Creek doesn't have a party circuit."

"It's summer, and there's nothing to do in this town

except drink and make out. I guarantee there's a party circuit." She takes another pull on her straw. "Once you and I hook up with the right people, we'll be set for the rest of the summer."

"Laurel, I don't—"

"Hey, loser, get off your lazy ass!" a male voice yells through the speaker. "We want to order some food."

I dive for the headset, knocking my stool over in the process, and Laurel chokes on her soda. "Sorry about that," I gasp into the speaker. "How may I please your taste buds today?"

"Cut the crap," the jackass in the car snarls. "We want three Cokes—the biggest size you got. And three large orders of fries."

There's something obnoxiously familiar about the voice on the other end of the intercom, but I'm too flustered to check the screen. "That's three jumbo Coke Washouts and three jumbo Flatcars." After I tell him the price and ask him to pull forward, I pour the drinks while Laurel gets the fries.

By then the rusty car has pulled up to the window. The milkshake I just drank comes halfway up my throat at the sight of Kong's bulging eyes and sloped forehead behind the wheel. I croak, "That'll be twelve dollars and seventy-three cents," and wait for the trash talk to start flying.

I grit my teeth as I take the twenty-dollar bill and hand

him his change. When nothing happens, I realize he doesn't recognize me with my hair tucked under the Sub Stop cap. Whew! Now I just have to hand off the food and drinks.

"Aspen, here are the fries," Laurel announces from behind me. I whirl around, frantically motioning her to be quiet. "Er . . . I mean Flatcars."

But it's too late. Ferret hangs his pointy muzzle out the rear window. "Hey, Kong, don't you recognize those bitches, Leaf Mold and Bark Rot?"

Kong takes a break from digging his finger into his ear. "Hey, yeah, it is them. Those stupid hats make them look even uglier than usual."

Without a word, I hand Kong the order. Buster, who's in the passenger seat, hasn't spoken, which makes me more uncomfortable. Before he can come up with a scintillating remark to top Ferret's and Kong's, I move away from the window. For much too long the car sits in the drivethrough, and I wonder what their microscopic minds are plotting.

When Kong finally pulls away, Laurel slams her hands on the counter. "Crap on toast! Now those losers know we work here!"

"So?" I ask while she's running cold water over her red palms. "They're the ones who have to worry."

Laurel turns off the water and pats her hands dry. "How do you figure?"

"Because if they piss us off, we can spit in their food—or worse."

"You wouldn't!" Laurel gapes at me with a mixture of horror and respect.

"Maybe, maybe not, but they're dense enough to believe we would."

She wraps me in a rib-crushing hug. "Aspen Parks, I've never been prouder to be your friend!"

"Okay, that's enough." My headset beeps and I pry her off me. "Somebody's at the menu board." I say my usual spiel into the microphone.

"One jumbo root beer Washout with no ice." The voice is oddly high-pitched, like a guy trying to sound female.

I squint at the static-filled screen, trying to make out the person slouched behind the wheel. Only one person I know has a face that doughy. I cover the microphone with my hand. "They're back, but Buster's driving now," I whisper to Laurel. "What's going on?"

"Fire in the hole." Laurel shakes her head grimly.

Now is not the time to be cryptic. "Huh?"

"Just do what I tell you," she says. "I'll explain later."

Laurel hands me a cup. "Fill it as full as you can, and jam the lid on tight. Make sure you give Buster his change before you hand him the drink." She's talking so fast I can barely understand her. "And this is the most important part: the very second the drink is in his

116

hand you have to dive away from the window. The very
second. Got it?"

I nod. Now I'm remembering "fire in the hole" from
YouTube a couple of years ago. Although I don't know
what Laurel has in mind, I'm all for not getting a face full
of root beer.

When Buster pulls up to the window, his face is impas-
sive and he's still being eerily silent. But Kong and Ferret
are acting like the snickering douches I've come to know
and despise.

I put Buster's money in the register and take my time
filling the cup. Meanwhile Laurel has squatted beneath the
window with her head just below the sill. Her hair is tick-
ling my bare knee, and I try to wriggle away from her.

"Don't lean out the window," Laurel whispers loudly.
"Make him come to you."

That's a disgusting thought. But I do what she says,
and Buster has to stretch out the car window to reach his
drink.

"Now!"

As I hurl myself away from the window, Laurel jumps
up and slides it shut. There's a colossal splat followed by
screams of profanity. When I look through the splattered
order window, I see Buster with root beer dripping down
his contorted face. He's sputtering and cursing and pounding his fists on the dashboard.

Almost as good is the sight of Ferret in the backseat trying to make himself invisible. No need to guess who came up with the idea to douse me with root beer. And who's going to get his butt kicked because of it.

I hate it when I forget to bring my cell phone to work.

eleven

FOR THE NEXT FEW DAYS, THE ENCOUNTER WITH BUSTER AND company satisfies Laurel's need for excitement. But by the weekend, she's back to singing her endless tune about getting us noticed.

"Come on, Aspen, it's already June twelfth, and we haven't hit a single party. Manny goes out all the time. Can't he get us invited?"

"He probably could, if he wanted to." I set a stack of cups by the drink machine. "But he's still pissed about his graduation omelet. Or so he says. Mostly he just doesn't want me at the same parties he goes to."

"That's stupid. It's not like you'd hang around him." Laurel drags a wet cloth around the floor with her foot.

We're supposed to use the mop for spills, but that only happens when Willie's watching. "Now, *I'd* hang as close to him as I possibly could." She sighs. "He still hasn't hooked up with anyone, has he?"

Knowing Manny, he's hooking up as often as humanly possible, but Laurel doesn't need to hear that. "Manny doesn't exactly confide in me, but I don't think so, especially since he's going to Iowa State at the end of August."

A car pulls up to the menu board. "I've got this one," Laurel says as she snatches up the headset. "Welcome to the Sub Stop, hot stuff," she coos in a tone so sultry the bread delivery guy behind her nearly swallows his tongue. "How may I tempt your taste buds today?"

There's a pause on the other end of the intercom. Then a male voice answers, "Let me get back to you on that when my kids aren't in the car. For now I'll just have a Barn Burner special and two chicken Cabooses."

When Laurel finishes entering the order, I turn on her. "What was that? The only women who talk that way are charging two ninety-nine a minute."

She shrugs. "I'm just trying to liven things up a little."

"By getting arrested for being a smut-monger?"

"There's no smut involved," Laurel says. The car pulls up to the window, and she hands the bag of sandwiches to a chubby, middle-aged guy with a receding hairline and an eager smile on his flushed face. When she leans halfway out the window and purrs, "Thank you, and have a delightful day," he looks like he's about to stroke out.

"My God, Laurel, that's disgusting!"

"He didn't think so." She smiles. "And he'll be back. I guarantee it."

"Either that or he'll be waiting to jump you in the parking lot after we close. Listen, if you want to liven things up, say something funny to the kids in the car." Anything is better than Smut Girl.

Thankfully the next customer is an older woman, and Laurel plays it straight. After that is a mom with three little kids. "Hewwo. Our special today is the wascally wabbit sandwich." Her Elmer Fudd isn't half bad. "Would you like to order thwee of those?"

When the mom drives up to the window, she's smiling even though her kids are bouncing in their car seats, demanding to see Elmer and Bugs. For the rest of our shift, Laurel keeps the headset clamped on and refuses to switch with me when it's my turn to take orders. I don't mind so much when she's trying out her cartoon voices. But she still uses her two-ninety-nine-a-minute voice on every male customer who drives through.

And even though the customers all leave smiling, I'm sure this voice thing is going to blow up in her face.

★ ★ ★

Tuesday is our day off. After I take Carmine for his morning walk and check my Facebook news feed, I'm at a loss for something to do. When I think it's late enough for Laurel to be awake, I call and ask if she wants to go for a bike ride along the Raccoon River Valley Trail. She's still laughing when she hangs up on me. Undaunted, I decide to fly in the face of convention and ride alone.

It's a beautiful June morning with scattered clouds and a light breeze. The temperature is just above seventy degrees, and the humidity hasn't kicked in. Now that I'm on my bike, having some alone time doesn't seem like a bad thing. I'll ride across town and catch the trail where it runs through the city park. The first mulberries should be getting ripe. Even if they're not ready yet, I'm positive the wild serviceberries are. This early in the morning, there shouldn't be anyone around to see me filling my face with fruit or to make fun of my purple tongue. Maybe it's a good thing Laurel didn't want to come with me. Last fall she was horrified when I ate a crabapple straight off the tree in our backyard. "Aren't you going to wash it first?" she gasped. "Bugs have probably pooped all over it!" Like possible bug poop is worse than the pesticides on the fruit they sell at the grocery store.

"Aspen Parks, I'm talking to you! Didn't your parents teach you that it's rude to ignore people?"

No. Life can't be that cruel. But Miss Simmons is standing on her front porch, shaking her wrinkled fist at me.

Since there's no way out now, I jump the curb and steer my bike onto her front walk. "I'm sorry, Miss Simmons. I didn't hear you."

She snorts. "A girl your age should have perfect hearing. If you kids didn't listen to that shouting nonsense on the radio, you'd—"

"You're absolutely right, Miss Simmons," I cut in, "and that's why I'm going for a nice, quiet ride in the country."

"Hmph!" She peers up and down the street. "Before you go riding off, you need to do something for me. This blasted hip replacement is taking forever to heal, and the cold, damp weather is making it act up even worse."

My scalp feels sweaty under my helmet. "I'm sorry to hear that."

Miss Simmons makes another nervous sweep with her eyes. What's she doing, selling contraband laxatives?

"With this hip bothering me, I haven't been able to take Sammy Stripers on his walks. The poor little fellow is getting restless."

"You take him out on a leash? Aren't you afraid somebody will see him?"

Miss Simmons looks at me over the tops of her glasses. "Your brother was blessed with the looks in the family. I thought you might have gotten the brains." She shakes her head. "Of course Sammy doesn't walk. He rides in his stroller."

What was I thinking? People everywhere push their pet skunks around in strollers.

"So, what are you waiting for?" she demands. "The stroller is here on the porch, and Sammy's in his crate. He prefers to have his walks around sunrise, but since you're here so late he'll have to make do."

No way.

"Miss Simmons, you aren't . . . You can't be . . . You don't really expect me to push your pet skunk around the neighborhood in a stroller . . . do you?"

"Why not?" She stumps across the porch behind her walker. "You'll get fresh air and exercise—it might even brighten up your sallow complexion. It's a pity when a girl your age has such drab coloring."

This is my only day off this week, and I want to ride my bike. Why should I let her boss me around? "Wait a minute, Miss Simmons. I haven't agreed to take Sammy for a walk. And, to be honest, I don't want to."

Miss Simmons doesn't even break hobble. "Is that so? Well then, little Miss I Don't Want To, I'll have to tell your parents about you and your flashy redheaded friend out gallivanting until four o'clock in the morning a few weeks ago. Naturally I won't want to. . . ."

Why am I being punished? Was I a serial killer in a previous existence?

"Okay, you win." I prop my bike against the porch and steer the stroller out of the corner. From the looks of this thing, Miss Simmons probably rode in it when she was a kid a hundred years ago. The wheels wobble and creak with age. When I shake dust off the sun-bleached cover, I can see daylight through it. "Once around the block, and I don't have to touch him."

"I've already promised him two times." Miss Simmons lowers herself into a padded rocker. "Carry his crate out here and I'll show you how to get him out."

So much for my demands. "He's been fixed, right?"

"Of course, he's been neutered," she says indignantly. "And I give him rabies and distemper shots every year."

"That's not the kind of fixed I'm talking about. Has his . . . stinker been destunk?"

"Absolutely not! That's Sammy's natural protection."

My hand freezes on her front doorknob. "What's to stop him from spraying me?"

"As long as you don't expose him to dogs, cats, or loud noises and don't make any sudden movements, you should be fine. And if anyone comes near, put the top up and tell them the baby is asleep." Miss Simmons motions me to go into the house. "Just remember, if he lifts his tail and stamps, you've upset him, and you'd be well-advised to move at least ten feet away."

Getting Sammy out of his crate was surprisingly easy. After he sniffed my fingers, he toddled into my waiting hands and let me lift him into the stroller. Except for his sharp toenails, he seems harmless. I was worried he might jump out of the stroller, but Miss Simmons says it won't be a problem. His skunk eyesight is so awful that he'd be afraid to jump without knowing where he would land.

Except for feeling like an idiot, I'm having fun pushing Sammy. He's a handsome little guy, with coarse black fur and white stripes that run from one end to the other. And it's cute the way he rests his little front paws on the rim of the stroller and swivels his head back and forth, his black nose twitching nonstop.

We're on our second trip around the block. After the first time around, Miss Simmons made me push him up her sidewalk so she could make sure he was enjoying himself. While she was cooing and scratching Sammy behind the ears, I almost forgot what an old witch she is.

A horn honks on the street beside me, three friendly beeps like someone saying hello. I check Sammy to make sure the noise hasn't freaked him out before looking over to see who's honking. When I see Clay's dark green pickup pull up to the curb, my heart does backflips.

"Hey, Aspen. I thought that was you." Clay cuts the engine, pushes his baseball cap back, and leans his forearm on the open window. "Manny said you're working at the Sub Stop. But you're babysitting, too?"

Sammy cocks his head toward the sound of Clay's voice. "Uh . . . no . . . I mean yes." I fumble to lift the top of the stroller before Clay sees what's inside. Naturally, the stupid thing is stuck. I jerk the cover, the stroller lurches, and Sammy starts chattering in an unhappy way.

If Sammy's unhappy, there's a good chance that nobody's going to be happy.

"Hold on a sec," Clay says as he climbs out of his truck. "I'll help you."

"That's okay. I can get it." I grab the cover with both hands and yank. The fabric splits with a nasty-sounding rip, and my bony butt slams onto the sidewalk. Agony shoots up my spine, and I taste blood.

Through tears of pain, I see the stroller rolling away. Even worse, Clay is running behind it, reaching for the handle.

"Don't, Clay! Skunk!" With the wind knocked out of me, all that comes out is a gasp. I watch in horror as Clay drags the stroller to a standstill. He's going to get blasted with skunk spray, and there's nothing I can do to stop it.

My tailbone is splintered into at least a thousand pieces, probably crippling me for life. Despite the blinding pain, I struggle to my feet and speed-hobble toward the impending disaster.

"Okay, not what I expected." Clay backs away from the stroller. He turns, sees me struggling, and slides his arm around my waist to support me. "Sorry I didn't help you up, but I thought it was a baby."

"Most people would." I wrap my left arm around Clay's firm middle and let him hold me up. My rear still hurts, but the rest of me is feeling better. Much better. "I tried to warn you, but I couldn't catch my breath."

"The little guy must be used to people," Clay says. "Otherwise, I'd have gotten a world of hurt in the eyes." He helps me take the few steps to the stroller. When I look in, Sammy's sitting calmly with his front paws folded.

"Yeah, he's tamer than I thought." I lean into Clay's side. "But I'm no skunkologist."

"Understandable," Clay deadpans. "Skunkologists are a rare breed." He lets Sammy sniff the back of his free hand. Then he scratches him behind the ears. "I take it he's not yours?"

"No, he belongs to my neighbor, Miss Simmons. She had her hip replaced and can't take him out." Then I remember why I was trying to cover Sammy. "Please don't mention him to anyone. I guess keeping skunks as pets isn't legal, and she's worried somebody will turn her in."

Clay removes his arm from my waist. "First you lie to an officer of the law. Now you're concealing illegal wildlife. What's next—smuggling drugs?"

My face sizzles with embarrassment. "I . . . It's not . . ."

He laughs. "Relax. I'm just giving you a hard time. It's great that you're giving your neighbor a hand."

I duck my head modestly. This is not the time to tell Clay

how Miss Simmons blackmailed me. I change the subject. "So, what are you doing here?" It comes out sounding more like an interrogation than a casual comment.

"I was on my way to your house. Manny said his engine is running rough, and he asked me to take a look at it before work."

So much for my fantasy that Clay came by to see me.

Sammy has his front paws back on the edge of the stroller, and his head is swiveling like a weathervane. "I think your buddy's impatient to get back on the road," Clay says.

Stupid weasel. "I guess so." I fold down the ripped cover as well as I can. Miss Simmons will have plenty to say about that.

My one chance to talk to Clay, and I'm chauffeuring a stink bomb. "Well, thanks."

The cool person always leaves first, so I nudge the stroller a baby step forward. I don't want to intimidate Clay by seeming too cool.

"How's your . . . uh . . . back?" he asks.

"It's all right." I bravely take another pain-wracked step.

"You know what? I can help you finish your walk and still have time to give Manny a hand with his car." Clay slips his arm around my waist again. "Or if you're in too much pain, I can load the stroller into the truck and drive you."

I mold myself against his ribs like Play-Doh. "With you helping me, I'm sure I can make it. I did promise Miss Simmons."

With one arm around each other and steering with our free hands, Clay and I push Sammy along the sidewalk.

For the first time I realize the benefits of working through the pain.

twelve

THAT AFTERNOON, LAUREL AND I ARE SITTING IN LOUNGE chairs on my deck. She's holding a hand mirror and twisting herself into a pretzel to admire the new henna swan tattoo on her left shoulder blade. "Did he kiss you? Grope your ass? Declare his undying love? I need details!"

"None of the above. It was broad daylight, and we were taking a skunk for a walk." I shift the bag of frozen peas from my numb tailbone to my left butt cheek. Thanks to my dismal social life, no one will see the ugly multi-colored bruises.

"About that." Laurel lays the mirror on the patio table and sinks back into the lounger. "Did Miss Simmons freak when she discovered that Clay knew her deep, dark secret?"

"Not at all." I smile, remembering how Miss Simmons kept forcing lemonade and cookies on Clay. He had to back out her door to escape. "I thought she was going to have adoption papers drawn up. According to her, Sammy's an excellent judge of character, and it was practically a sign from heaven that he didn't squirt skunk juice all over Clay."

"I'm sure Clay was thrilled." Laurel picks up her tube of sunblock and squeezes some onto her legs. "Speaking of thrilling news, we're invited to a kick-ass party Saturday night," she says as if we're kick-ass party regulars.

Her comment may be carefree, but her eyes are shifty. "Really? Who invited us?"

"It's at an old barn in the country that has . . . something upstairs with hay in it."

"A hayloft?"

"That's it," Laurel agrees, watching lotion sink into her legs. "So, what exactly is hay? And why do farmers keep it upstairs instead of on the ground?"

Laurel's trying to distract me, but I like knowing something she doesn't. "Hay is made of alfalfa or clover. When the alfalfa gets ripe, farmers cut it off, rake it up, and let it dry in the field. When it's dry enough, they use a machine to make it into bales." I resist the urge to pat myself on the back. "The bales are put into a hayloft to keep them dry. In the winter farmers feed the hay to their cows and horses."

"Really?" Laurel actually looks impressed. "So how do you know all that?"

"My uncle George and aunt Carol have a farm near Iowa City. When I was twelve, I stayed with them for a week during the summer and helped with the chores. One of the chores was to pick up hay bales." I check the bag of peas for leaks. So far, so good. "Now let's get back to talking about the party."

"It's only for seniors—which we are, of course—and grads. So no dorky underclassmen."

I know her too well to let her throw me off track again. "So who did you say invited us?"

Laurel is rubbing lotion between her toes. "Tessa called me," she mumbles without looking up.

I throw up a little in my mouth. "Are you serious? Tessa Chandler called you and invited *both of us* to a party?"

"Why not?" Laurel's wandering eye is twitching like a strobe light.

"Why not? I can think of a million reasons, but if you give me a few minutes I'll come up with more." I sit up, wincing as I crush a clump of frozen peas under my tailbone. "So what prompted Tessa to add *us* to her social circle?"

"She heard some guys talking about the way I take orders at the Sub Stop, and unlike some people"—she pauses—"Tessa thinks using a sexy voice is very cool."

Now there's a shocker.

"Speaking of the Sub Stop," I say, choosing to ignore Laurel's attitude, "we have to work until nine o'clock on Saturday. That's pretty late to be riding our bikes in the country."

"Ride our bikes! That's social suicide!" The look of horror on her face is priceless. "Tessa and Wynter are going to pick us up after work."

Aha! "So you accepted for both of us without asking me first?"

"So sorry not to have consulted you." Laurel peers at me. "What event on your busy social schedule will you have to cancel?"

I bite my tongue and adjust the bag of peas.

Score one for Laurel.

Saturday night Tessa and Wynter pull up to the Sub Stop at five minutes after nine in Wynter's bright red slut-mobile. Since I fully expected them to leave us waiting like naïve fools, I'm forced to give them a point for following through.

They're all smiles at Laurel, complementing her low-rise denim shorts, yellow halter top, and the brown henna swan above her shoulder blade. The cloak of invisibility hides my navy tee, khaki shorts, and me. Tessa and Wynter manage to act as if I'm not in the car—or on the planet.

As soon as we take off, Tessa turns around in the passenger seat. "Now remember what I told you about working the party, Laurel. It's okay to touch base with each other once in a while, but guys don't like to approach clumps of girls—especially if one of them is a loser. No guy wants to get stuck with the dead weight."

Tessa should give herself a little more credit. Just because I think she's dead weight doesn't mean everyone does.

"If you hook up, let one of us know before you head out," she continues. "We don't want to waste time trying to find you when we're ready to go." For the first time she looks at me. "I'll nod at you or something. Wait for us by the car."

Enough is enough.

I lean against the back of Wynter's seat and gush, "Ooh, let's work out a super-secret 'time to go' signal. One finger up your nose means we leave in five minutes, and two fingers means ten."

Tess curls her upper lip at me. Too bad there isn't spinach stuck between her teeth. "Don't get too wasted, either," she says to Laurel. "Being super-drunk is tacky."

Tessa's lecture on coolness continues, but now I'm fearing for my life. Wynter is blasting down the unmarked, pitch-black gravel roads, taking corners like a NASCAR driver. My death-grip on the armrest is all that keeps me from crashing into Laurel. I can't believe how relaxed and smiling she is, with her hands resting in her lap.

When Tessa finally turns back around, I scoot across the seat and whisper into Laurel's ear. "You're not going along with this 'work the party' crap are you? I only agreed to come because you said we'd stay together."

"Of course we'll stay together," she whispers back. "Maybe not 'together, together' but definitely 'together.'"

"What does that—"

Wynter screeches around a corner, hurling me into the driver's-side door and Laurel into me. The car's rear end fishtails, slamming us against each other again. I squeeze my eyes shut and brace for a collision.

"Wynter, slow the hell down!" Tessa shrieks. "Farmer Boy isn't worth dying over!"

Farmer Boy? No, it can't be. There are thousands of farmers in Iowa. Then I flash back to Manny's graduation party and Wynter's tongue groping for Clay's ear.

My eyes fly open, but the night is blacker than ever and I see nothing but trees. Wynter backs off the gas as we bounce down a rutted path that's nearly overgrown with weeds. It's a good thing she's driving us home, because I have no idea where we are.

After a few minutes of us bumping through the dark, the trees open into a clearing packed with cars. Wynter parks between a muddy pickup and a muddier SUV, both of which look as if they drove up a creek to get here. I guess it has rained a lot this week.

As soon as we're out of the car, Tessa links arms with Wynter and Laurel, leaving me to walk behind them. The worst part is that they look perfectly natural together, like three exotic parrots on the same perch. And I'm the sparrow on the floor of the cage, getting crapped on.

The barn door is only a quarter of the way open, which means they have to break apart to go inside. Laurel falls back with me. "Don't let them get to you, Aspen. You and I are going to have an awesome time tonight."

It's almost as dark inside the barn as outside. A few gas lanterns hanging along the far wall backlight the people standing in clusters and sitting on hay bales. I hear the rumble of bass in the background music, but the volume is turned down.

Laurel stops by the door and scans the huge, open area. "What's going on? Why's everybody so quiet?"

"Cops." Wynter squints into the semi-darkness. "They've got nothing better to do on the weekend than cruise around, looking for parties to bust." She shifts her boobs to a higher elevation. "So we have to find quiet ways to keep busy."

"I think you mean 'get busy,'" Tessa says. She and Wynter exchange a leer that would even make Ferret flinch. With their hips swaying like pigs in a gunnysack, they sashay off in search of unsuspecting males.

As I watch them disappear into the dark, my skin crawls. "You seriously want to be friends with those two?"

Laurel's quiet for a moment. Then she shakes her head. "For two seconds I thought I did. But that's not the kind of popularity I want." She links arms with me. "Come on. Let's see what this party has to offer."

The barn smells of spilled beer, cigarettes, and weed layered over the dusty smell of pigeon droppings. The combination of odors in the heat makes my mouth pucker and my tongue curl. As my eyes grow used to the dark, I recognize several girls from my class. Laurel and I exchange hellos with them but keep shuffling forward to see who we can see.

Tessa's "farmer boy" remark still has me frazzled, and I pull up short at every tall guy who looms out of the darkness. There's no sign of Clay, which is disappointing. But at least he hasn't hooked up with Wynter. Not yet, anyway.

Laurel stops us by the keg where Sam and Tyler, who I've known since kindergarten, are manning the tap. "Would miladies care to partake of some brewskis?" With a goofy smile, Sam holds out a foaming paper cup like a kid flying a paper airplane. His eyelids can't seem to make it more than halfway up.

Sam asked me to the Winter Wonderland Ball in February, but I turned him down for two reasons. First, I knew he'd asked five girls before he got to me. And second, he called me the morning of. I do have some standards.

"Thanks." Laurel snags the beer from Sam's wobbly hand and takes a drink. I pass. To me, beer looks and smells like something you bring to the doctor's office in a jar.

"Come on, then. We have to work the party," Laurel says in a spot-on Tessa imitation that cracks me up.

It doesn't seem like much of a party. The music is barely audible, and everyone's talking in hushed voices. I get more excitement reading in bed with Carmine's head resting on my thigh. At least he snores once in a while.

"This is what everyone raves about?" I whisper so as not to wake the dearly departed.

"I don't get it," Laurel whispers back. "There was better entertainment last winter at Great-aunt Evelyn's seventieth birthday party. Cuter guys, too."

"Does anyone in here have a pulse?" a guy shouts from the open barn door. "Charge up the paddles, because this party's coming to life!" His voice sounds disturbingly familiar.

Laurel and I look at each other and gasp, "Buster," just before he, Ferret, and Kong stomp by. They're loaded down with bulging plastic bags and an oversize cooler like the ones Mom borrowed for Manny's graduation party. Luckily they don't notice us in the dark.

"Do you think Buster's still pissed about getting drenched with pop?" Laurel asks.

"Nah." I pull her in the opposite direction from where they went. "Buster's not one to hold a grudge. Tear off a limb, gouge out an eye, but not hold a grudge."

"That's a fun fact." Laurel drains the last of her beer. "If I'm going to be blinded and dismembered, I'll need more than one beer to dull the pain." She makes a beeline for the keg, and—not wanting to be left behind—I follow her.

As we're walking, Tessa reaches out of the dark and grabs Laurel's arm. "Hey! How's it going?" She's leaning against a stocky, brown-haired guy I don't recognize. Her lipstick is smeared and her eyes are out of focus. "Are you having fun? I am."

Before Laurel can answer, Tessa lifts her head and kisses the guy behind her. Then she turns around, shoves her tongue down his throat, and grinds her hips against him. I pull Laurel away before Tessa's flying bra hits one of us.

"Back for seconds, I see." Sam, who's obviously been drinking as much as he's been serving, needs several tries to position the tap over Laurel's cup. Beer overflows onto their hands. When Sam tries to lick beer off her hand, she backs out of reach.

My mouth is parched, but not enough that I'll stoop to beer.

"Hey, Aspen." Sam tilts his head as if he's trying to remember what he was saying. "Hey, Aspen, since you don't like beer . . . you might . . . maybe you'd . . . like this punch." He reaches for a plastic milk jug on the floor and almost falls on his face. Finally, he squats, picks it up with both hands, and sets it on the keg.

"I hear it's fruity-licious," Tyler chimes in. His face is shiny with sweat, and there are huge damp rings around his neck and under the arms of his T-shirt. "Fruity-licious," he says again. He and Sam snicker.

Fruity sounds better than *urine sample*, so I take the jug from Sam, pour some of the red stuff into a cup, and sniff it. It smells like Hawaiian Punch. Tastes like it too— a little too sweet with kind of an aftertaste. But it's nice and cold.

I drain the cup and pour myself a refill. "What's in here?"

Sam shakes his head and only stays upright by holding on to the keg.

Tyler shrugs. "Probly Kool-Aid, ginger ale, fruit juice . . ."

Laurel tips the jug to her lips and drinks. "More like rocket fuel. Take it easy with that stuff."

"Hey, that's nasty!" I snatch the jug away from her, wipe off the top with my shirttail, and replace the cap. Just for that, I'm not going to mention the pink ring it left around her mouth.

"I'm serious, Aspen." Laurel tries to take the jug from

me, but I hide it behind my back. "Back in Chicago, kids dumped everything from their parents' liquor cabinets into the punch and called it jungle juice. That's probably what you're drinking."

"Jungle juice is a funny name. I wonder what it means." I swish the next mouthful around before I swallow. It tastes pretty good. "But I think you're wrong about the alcohol."

Laurel frowns at me over her beer. "Just drink it slow, okay?"

Music blasts from invisible speakers. The barn explodes with hoots and whistles. Sam and Tyler applaud. The sudden energy in the room hits me like a lightning bolt.

My hips sway with the music. My head bobs. My long, sexy legs ache to move. "Come on, Laurel. Let's dance."

She stares at me. "You hate dancing. You've told me at least a thousand times."

"Tonight I don't." I don't care if this punch is made of rubbing alcohol. I feel beautiful and graceful and so sexy.

My cup is empty again. The lid of the jug is stuck, but I finally twist it off and pour more punch into my cup. It tastes very wonderful.

Dancing feels very wonderful, too. I'm going to dance every day from now on. Sam is staring at me. Too bad for you, buddy. You missed your chance to dance with me. Chance to dance. That's a poem. I'm good at poems. I can write songs and chor . . . choreo . . . make up dances for them.

Laurel doesn't look like she's having much fun. She's hardly even moving her arms. She needs to loosen up. I should give her some of my punch.

I am so thirsty. It's good I left the lid off the thing because my fingers are fumbly. The floor is kind of tilting, probly 'cause it's an old barn. Hey, my punch is almost gone! Who's been drinking it?

No matter. I'll get some more.

I fling my hair over my shoulder like a rock star. "Isn't this fun?"

Laurel isn't dancing. She's staring at the door. With her eyes all wide, she looks like a raccoon in a tree.

"Laurel, you have a funny look—"

She grabs my arm and jerks me. "Aspen, let's get out of here!"

I jerk back. "Ouch! Don't pull so hard."

She jerks me again even harder. "Come on!" She sounds mad.

"I don't want to. I'm having fun."

Laurel holds my arms tight. "Aspen, try to focus." She's talking into my face. Her nose looks so wide, and her breath smells like beer. "A police car pulled up in front of the barn. We have to find another way out."

My stomach makes a loud sound, and a bitter taste boils

into my throat. I drink the rest of my punch to wash it down.

"Do you want to go to jail, Aspen?"

No, I don't. When I move my head back and forth, Laurel's face goes out of focus. She looks funny.

"Good." Laurel nods her head. I think. "Now walk with me. And don't talk to anybody."

She hooks her arm into my arm. She walks really fast, and I trip over stuff in the dark. Somebody swears at me, which is not very nice. I didn't kick that girl on purpose. But I want to now.

We're almost to the back of the barn when Kong's big body lurches in front of us. He has an ugly smile. "Look, Buster. It's Ass-wipe and Limp-tits."

"That's a mean thing to say. You always say mean things to us." I shove Kong in the stomach.

"Hey!" He shoves me back, but Laurel catches me before I fall.

"Forget him, Aspen." She's got my left arm again. "Let's get you some fresh air."

I dig in my heels. "I don't want fresh air. I want to see Kong get arrested."

Laurel slaps her hand over my mouth. Her hand is all sweaty. "Ignore her. She's drunk." She pulls on my arm.

Kong grabs my right arm. "Hold on! What's she talking about?"

I don't like being pulled apart like a wishbone. "The police are coming in the front door to arrest you," I tell Kong. It serves him right.

From the corner of my eye, I see flashlights swarming through the barn door like fireflies. "See! There they are!"

Everything happens at once. Kong drops my arm; Laurel yanks me hard toward the back wall. Because of the lanterns, it's lighter here, and I see the outline of a door in the corner. Laurel runs toward it, and I try to keep up.

All around us girls are screaming. People crash into each other, swear, turn around, and crash into other people. Someone shouts orders through a bullhorn, but nobody listens.

Laurel shoves the door open with her shoulder and pushes me outside. The cool air feels nice on my sweaty face. It smells good, too.

"Don't stand there, Aspen! Run!"

"Run where?" The ground feels wobbly, but that's silly. Ground doesn't wobble.

Laurel looks left and right like she's watching a tennis match. She points left. "That way!"

She takes off really fast. I don't want her to leave me, so I run after her. Hey, I'm fast, too. Faster than a deer. My feet are flying over the ground, and I'm not even out of breath. I could run a marathon. I could run two marathons back to back. I could run—

Oof! Why am I on the ground? Squishy, gritty mud is in my mouth and on my hands.

"Aspen, are you okay?" Laurel pulls me up by the armpits. "I think you tripped over that log."

I can't see a log, but it's darker than night, which is silly because it is night. It can't be darker than what it is.

"You scraped your knee. It's bleeding."

"I'm okay." My knee doesn't hurt, but my head feels thick and the trees look blurry. The punch in my stomach is sloshing.

Laurel bends down and touches my knee. "It doesn't look too bad. Can you walk okay? We need to get as far away as possible."

I wipe my eyes and look around. I don't see the barn, just trees—and weeds. Tall, thick, tangled weeds. "Where are we?"

"I have no idea." Laurel brushes dirt from her arm. "But I guess we'll come to a road eventually."

"All right."

Laurel will figure it out. She figures everything out.

With Laurel taking the lead, we duck around tangled shrubs, catch our toes on branches, and push through chest-high weeds. After a while, I don't feel strong and powerful anymore. I feel bruised and beat up and sick to my stomach. And scared.

"What if the police are waiting on the road?"

146

Laurel shrugs. "I don't know. They didn't see us drinking, so maybe we're okay."

"But what if they make us take breath tests?"

She bends a tall weed and smashes it flat with her foot. "We can't get caught. That's all."

Good deal. At least it's something easy.

thirteen

AFTER TEN OR A HUNDRED MINUTES, LAUREL AND I STAGGER TO the top of a hill and stop to catch our breath. From here I can still see the flickering red and blue lights of the police cars parked by the barn. But my stomach flips like a spinning disk of pizza dough when I see the smaller, fainter lights fanning out through the woods and fields.

"What are we going to do, Laurel? The police are chasing us!" Terror sucks at my breath. "If they catch us . . ." It's too horrible to put into words.

Laurel's round face hardens into grim lines. "They won't." She grabs my hand and squeezes it. "Let's go."

Hand in hand we hurl ourselves downhill, away from the flickering lights. Raspberry canes tear at my bare legs and leave long, fiery scratches. Hundreds of burrs poke into my new tee and shorts. Heat sears my lungs, and my breath comes in sobs that tear at my throat. I trip and catch myself, only to trip again.

We can't get caught. We can't get caught. We can't. We can't. The words pound in my head, keeping time with my running, stumbling feet.

My sandals slip on the soggy weeds and sink into the soft earth. The farther down the hill we run, the muddier it gets. Dampness clings to my face and arms, and I hear a wheezing, gurgling noise that's growing louder and louder.

By the time I realize what's making the noise, we're going too fast to stop. Momentum carries us into cold, murky creek water that smells like earthworms and other things that gave up on being alive a while ago. My feet try to slide in five directions at once, and in half a breath I'm sitting waist-deep in water.

Laurel, having a lower center of gravity, is still standing, although the water is sloshing up to her knees. She leans over and drags me to my feet. "OMG, Aspen! Did you get any of that water in your mouth?"

I shake my head no, but she keeps ranting. "You could catch typhoid or cholera or E. coli or—"

"Laurel! I didn't swallow any." Which doesn't rule out rampant infection from the bacteria-infested water seeping into the scratches on my arms and legs. "Just help me out of here."

With mud sucking at our shoes, we wade out of the creek and fight through the brambles on the opposite bank. My legs feel like dead stumps weighted down with cement. I do my best to protect my face from the lashing branches, but when they snap against my skin they bring tears to my eyes.

Laurel and I plod forward in no particular direction except away from the barn. One thing we have going for us is the moon, which is faintly visible through the clouds. If we keep it in front of us, we're not walking in circles. Are we?

Two flooded, nasty-smelling ditches later we slog onto a gravel road. We're coated with mud from the waist down and scratched everywhere else. Mosquitoes the size of great horned owls attack our arms and legs, and gnats swarm around our faces. The last ditch swallowed my left sandal, and I couldn't bring myself to feel around for it in the slime. Since then I've stepped on every thorn, stick, and pebble with my bare foot.

Laurel raises her arms in a victory salute. "Civilization at last!"

"If you say so." My stomach is getting queasier with every step, and a lumberjack is pounding his axe into my skull. All I see in either direction are stretches of deserted road with fields on either side. No houses, no lights, no nothing. "Any idea which way is Cottonwood Creek?"

"How should I know? You were born here." Laurel rubs the back of her hand across her cheek, leaving a long smear of mud. Her grimy shorts are barely hanging on her butt, and her halter top looks like she used it to mop the garage floor. I don't want to know how I look.

I check the cloudy sky, hoping to see some reflected light from Cottonwood Creek's courthouse or its three-block-long downtown district. It's possible that the sky looks a little lighter to my right. But maybe not. I could think better if my head stopped spinning.

Something wet plops on my head. I look up, and rain splashes in my eye.

"Crap on toast!" Laurel throws a full-body tantrum, foot stomping and all. "Now it's freaking raining!"

Standing here is getting us nowhere. "Town is this way." I take a right and start limping down the road. Even if we go the wrong direction, we'll find a house eventually.

After we've trudged through the rain for several minutes in dismal silence, Laurel says, "What do you think happened to Tessa and Wynter?"

I'm too miserable to care about anyone else, especially those two.

"They got caught; I know it," Laurel continues

without waiting for me to answer. Which I wasn't going to do, anyway. "The police probably blocked in all the cars. Hey, I'll bet Buttferk got caught, too."

Even that thought doesn't cheer me up.

The road in front of us gets lighter, but there's nothing ahead. When I hear the growl of an engine, I realize a car is coming up behind us. My first instinct is to grab Laurel and dive into the ditch. But my pounding head, throbbing foot, and bubbling stomach veto that plan.

I turn toward the light.

The car or alien craft or whatever is creeping along at grandpa speed. Either a hundred-year-old woman is driving or it's a pervert on the prowl. As long as it's dry inside—and if it ever gets to us—I'm in. But I hold on to Laurel's arm in case a chain saw swipes at us out the window and we have to run for it.

Manny starts yelling even before he pulls alongside us. "Aspen, that is you! What the hell are you doing out here?"

I have never, ever been so happy to hear my brother's annoying voice. The car is still moving when I yank open the passenger door and vault inside.

And land sideways in Clay's lap with a muddy splat.

He makes a huffing noise. I gasp. Then we sit in stunned silence while rainwater drips down my neck and the muck from my shorts oozes into his jeans.

The silence is short-lived.

"What have you been doing—mud wrestling?" Manny screeches. "Get your grimy ass out of my car!" He reaches across the seat and shoves me. Hard.

I brace my feet against the doorframe. "No way! It's raining. And Laurel and I are freezing."

"You can't leave them out here," Clay says. "We're at least five miles from town." But he doesn't return my smile of thanks.

Uttering a string of curses, Manny climbs out of his car and pops the trunk. He lifts out an armful of blankets and dumps them onto the backseat. "Spread those out before you get in. And I'd better not see a single drop of mud on my clean seats."

Since Laurel and I know how Manny feels about his precious car, we do what he says, even though rain is pelting our backs. We're so filthy that the rain can only help.

By the time we crawl into the backseat, we're soaked from head to toe and our teeth are chattering. Manny tosses a towel onto Laurel's lap, and I notice that Clay is using another towel to blot his jeans. It would be just my luck that I ruined his clothes.

"So, Manny, why are you guys driving around out here?" Laurel, who is much braver than I am, asks.

Manny snarls something unintelligible before he says, "Clay and I were on our way to check out a barn party when I got a text that the cops raided it. Since we missed the excitement, we decided to cruise around for people who are trying to get back to town."

He sneers at me in the rearview mirror. "And look who turned up on the idiot meter."

It's bad enough that Clay is seeing me like this without my brother making things worse. "Hey, we were smart enough not to get caught." Like I had anything to do with us getting away.

"How'd you get out there—by riding double on Aspen's bike?"

Running through muddy ditches must have soured Laurel's mood because she gives Manny the finger behind the seat back as she says, "Tessa and Wynter invited us, so we caught a ride with them."

I try to catch Clay's reaction to Wynter's name in the rearview mirror, but I can't see his face in the dark. So I'm no closer to knowing if he's the "farmer boy" Tessa was talking about.

At least Laurel's name-dropping shuts Manny up for the time being. Or maybe it's a coincidence, because right about then the sky opens up and throws rain at the car in fifty-gallon barrels.

While Manny steers down gravel roads that the pounding rain has turned into mud soup, Laurel and I take turns drying our hair with the towel he threw at us. He has enough towels and blankets in his trunk to open his own motel. Which leads to thoughts about my brother and his serial girlfriends that I'll need decades of therapy to erase.

Meanwhile, Manny has his hands full keeping his car on the road. Whenever he accelerates above a snail's pace, the back end swerves and shoots plumes of muddy water at the windows. The wipers thrash back and forth at top speed and smear long streaks of mud on the windshield. Manny is hunched over the steering wheel like an old man, but I can't imagine either of my grandpas using the words coming out of his mouth.

The deafening rain is crushing my skull, and the rocking seats and stagnant air are agitating the nasty brew in my stomach. I haven't been carsick since I was ten, but it's all coming back to me now. If I don't get some fresh air—

I manage to gasp, "Manny, stop the car! I'm going to throw up!" before I have to clamp both hands over my mouth.

"You puke and you die!" Manny jams on the brakes, throwing the car into a skid. Laurel and I bounce like Ping-Pong balls. And the gallon of punch I chugged rises like the tide.

As we lurch to a crosswise stop, I shove the door open and thrust my head and shoulders into the blinding rain. Spasms seize my insides, and the jungle juice—no longer fruity and delicious—burns my throat on its way out . . . and out . . . and out. Between heaves, I gasp for breath, but the air stinks like booze-laced vomit, twisting my stomach into more spasms.

After what seems like an hour of emptying my stomach, I draw a shuddering breath. Inch by inch I straighten up, pushing my sweat-and-rain-soaked hair out of my eyes. I try a few more breaths and decide I'm not going to throw up any more.

I'm wrong.

When I've finished puking again, I sink my butt onto the car floor and keep my head and feet out in the rain. My rib muscles throb, and my skull feels like it's cracking into a hundred pieces.

The light blinds me.

It's supposed to be a peaceful, soothing light that draws me in. Not true. It's a nasty, glaring light that burns into my eye sockets even when my eyes are closed. I can't see anyone beckoning me, which can't be right because my hamster, Mr. Puggles, definitely went to heaven.

"This is the Cottonwood Creek police! Get out of the car and keep your hands where I can see them!"

Okay, so it's possible I'm not dying after all. But this scenario may be worse.

Until Clay reaches down to help me up, I don't realize he's gotten out of the car. "Stand up, Aspen. You can lean on me."

I grab Clay's hands and wobble to my feet on jelly legs. The sky and ground are spinning in opposite directions, which makes it hard to keep my balance. Holding their hands in the air, Manny and Laurel get out on the other side of the car. Clay lets go of my hands and raises his, too. Rain drips off the end of his nose. Without his support, I sway a little before I get my balance.

As a luminous green figure approaches Manny, the same voice, though not nearly as loud or deep, asks for his license and registration. While Manny ducks back in the car to retrieve them, the glowing green person says, "So, tell me, what are you kids doing out here?"

Laurel peers at the face under the plastic-covered hat. "Officer Sierra?" Her hair is flattened against her skull, and her nipples are poking through her sopping halter top. She must realize it, too, because she crosses her arms over her chest.

He turns, and I recognize his broad face above the florescent green slicker he's wearing. "I am. Wait, you're Laurel, the wisecracker." Manny hands over his documents, and Officer Sierra looks at them—and us. "Sure, I remember all of you now. Which brings me back to my original question: 'What are all of you doing out here?'"

Manny clears his throat, and he and Clay exchange a look over the roof of the car. "Just riding around in the country. You know, for something to do."

Officer Sierra tips his hat to one side, and water pours off it. "Now, Manny, that's kind of hard for me to believe. You see, an hour or so ago we raided a keg party in an old barn a mile and a half from here. We rounded up most of the kids, but some of them slipped out the back door."

The officer's stare takes in Laurel's muddy legs. "You wouldn't happen to know anything about that, would you, Laurel? Because you look pretty rough for a girl who's been riding in a car all night."

Laurel swallows and wipes the rain off her face.

Officer Sierra saunters over to where Clay and I are standing. I'm doing my best to stand up straight, but my brain is taking a roller-coaster ride and my stomach is roiling like angry surf. "Aspen, isn't it? You look like death warmed over." He eyes the nasty puddle at my feet. Then he leans toward my face and sniffs. "Good Lord! You smell like rot-gut booze."

I clutch my stomach and spew jungle juice all over his shiny black shoes.

fourteen

THE LAWNMOWER ROARS INTO MY ACHING HEAD LIKE A chain saw. The vibrations plow up my trembling hands and through my ruined nervous system to what's left of my brain. The inside of my mouth is permanently coated with foul-tasting paste, and it's likely that my stomach has given up on food forever.

Mom and Dad dragged me out of bed at the butt crack of dawn and practically chained me to the lawnmower. If I survive this torture, I'm supposed to weed Mom's tomatoes. And the chores go on and on until I drop dead or the sun sets, whichever comes first.

A hand clamps onto my shoulder, and I drop the mower handle and spin around. The engine stops abruptly, and blessed silence ensues.

"Hey, you missed a spot back there," Manny says. He's dressed for work in khaki shorts and a white polo shirt. In addition to his golf clothes, he's wearing an obnoxious smirk. If I had the energy, I'd punch him.

"You don't look so good, Sis. Feeling a little rough around the edges?"

"Shut up." I wipe my sweaty face with the tail of my T-shirt. My skin, my clothes, even my hair, smell like recycled alcohol. When I finish today's indentured servitude, I'm going to stand in the shower until we run out of water.

"Being hungover sucks, doesn't it?" Manny's smirk grows into a full-fledged grin. "You know the saying, 'If you're gonna play, you gotta pay.'" He hands me an insulated cup. "Drink some of this. Sometimes it helps."

I sniff it suspiciously. "What's in it?"

"Traditional hangover cure." He shades his eyes with his hand. "Tomato juice, Tabasco, salt and pepper, raw egg. Same ingredients as the omelet you made for me, but without the Tums and Pepto. Go on, try it."

For once, my brother looks and sounds sincere. My first sip barely wets my tongue. The spicy saltiness tastes good, and I take a real drink. "Thanks." I stand perfectly still while the liquid slides into my stomach. "Of course, the true test is if it stays down." My insides gurgle to let me know they haven't decided yet.

Manny pulls a baseball cap out of his back pocket and puts it on. "So how long are you grounded?"

"Mom said six months, but Dad won't let her stick to it." *I hope.* "She's really pissed about having to come to the police station to pick me up."

After I barfed on Officer Sierra's shoes, he made each of us blow into his drunk-detector gadget. Since Manny and Clay hadn't been drinking, they passed with flying colors. Laurel's breath registered below the legal limit, which didn't mean squat because she's still underage. My level was so high that Officer Sierra considered calling an ambulance, but I convinced him that I'd barfed most of the alcohol out of my system.

He bundled Laurel and me into the back of his squad car. In case I wasn't humiliated enough, he made me carry an evil-smelling yellow plastic pail to catch any future offerings. With Manny and Clay following, he drove us to the station and called our parents. At the police station Laurel and I sat wrapped in towels on a hard wooden bench outside Officer Sierra's office. He told Manny and Clay they could go home if they wanted, but Manny said they'd stay until our parents got there. He and Clay sat on an identical bench across the hall, facing Laurel and me. Every now and then Manny looked over at me and shook his head. Clay just stared at the gray tiled floor.

Laurel's dad, who was the first to get to the station, seemed more sleepy than angry. He kept yawning while Officer Sierra explained where Laurel and I had been and why he picked us up. After Laurel said she'd only drunk part of one beer, I could tell her dad didn't think it was anything to get excited about. Mostly I got the feeling he wanted to get out of the police station before any of his bank customers came in for some reason and saw him there. I knew Laurel wanted to stay and see what my parents were going to do, but her dad dragged her off before they blew in.

Two minutes later, Mom stormed into the police station with wild-looking bed hair and wilder-looking eyes. There's nothing she hates more than to be embarrassed in public. And having your daughter hurl on a policeman's shoes ranks pretty high in embarrassing moments. The more Officer Sierra described what happened, the madder she got. Since my blood alcohol level was off the charts, I couldn't lie and say I'd had only half a drink. Mom yelled and lectured and threatened while I died of humiliation, knowing Clay was hearing every word. Dad sat beside Manny and let Mom rant for both of them. I think Dad felt kind of sorry for me, but he values his life too much to say anything.

The ride home was endless. Mom had moved beyond ranting to silent, seething rage. After asking me if I was okay, Dad kept quiet, too. I was a sick, soggy lump of misery shivering in the backseat. The minute we got home, Mom turned her back on me and stomped upstairs.

Dad waited until their bedroom door slammed shut. He patted my damp shoulder. "Take a hot shower, drink a big glass of water, and try to get some sleep. Your mom is pretty mad right now, but she'll calm down in a couple of days. Maybe I can talk to her about getting your sentence reduced." He rubbed his eyes. "But I'd strongly suggest that you avoid any parties for a good, long time."

Manny tucks his shirttail into his shorts. "Yeah, Mom and Dad look the other way about my partying, but it's different with you. And the police station thing was the icing on the cake, especially for Mom."

My stomach does a pirouette. "Don't mention food!"

"Been there." Manny gives me a knowing nod. "Is Mom going to make you quit your job?"

I sip some more of Manny's hangover cure. "No. She thinks working will keep me out of trouble. And I still have to walk Miss Simmons's sk—stupid cat."

"Yeah, Mom and Dad are heavy into the work ethic." He unhooks the sunglasses from the front of his shirt and slips them on. "Listen, Aspen, I'm in no position to lecture you about drinking. But that jungle juice is lethal. It's laced with Everclear, which will knock you on your ass." Manny clears his throat. "And guys make it taste good to get girls drunk and . . . well, you know."

I almost choke. "Thanks for the brotherly concern, Manny, but I'm the last girl anybody wants to hit on."

"My buddy Clay seems kind of interested." Manny scratches his head. "I can't imagine why."

My heart gives a happy jump, which dies immediately. "Last night took care of that."

Manny shrugs. "Guys generally aren't turned on by projectile vomiting, but you never know." He looks back at the house. "Uh-oh. A certain mother who shall remain nameless is giving us the death look. You'd better get back to it."

"I guess." As he starts across the lawn to his car, I add, "Hey, thanks for the magic potion."

He turns and touches his cap. "And I expect you to remember it when you make my next omelet."

All day Sunday Mom outdoes herself in inventing chores for me. Her fury is charged to maximum power. Dad sends me the occasional sympathetic look, but that's as far as it goes. I don't blame him. It wouldn't do either of us any good. I'm banned from talking to Laurel, and Manny doesn't come home until long after dark. I've never been so glad to see Monday morning.

"OMG, that party was such a bust." Laurel sighs and

props her elbows on the counter by the Sub Stop drive-up window. "I didn't meet one cute guy, the music was lame, and the beer wasn't even cold."

"Almost getting arrested wasn't that much fun, either." We're having the usual lull before the Monday noon rush at the Sub Stop. The day after my marathon of chores, my stomach is still yucky, but I'm beginning to believe there's hope for survival.

Laurel sets her jumbo soda under the spigot and tops it off. "At least if we'd been arrested, we could have bragged about it. Who wants to hear about getting off with a warning?"

"It was more than enough excitement for me." I shudder when I remember the look on Officer Sierra's face after I barfed on his shoes.

A car pulls up to the order screen, and Laurel grabs the headphones. "I've got it." She closes her eyes and coos, "Welcome to Sub Stop. How may I tempt your taste buds—or other erogenous zones—today?"

She rips off the headphones as if they're charged with electricity. They land on the counter with a whack as we hear an outraged screech from outdoors.

"What the hell, Laurel! Who is that?"

Laurel bites her lower lip. "I was thinking about Saturday night, and I forgot to look."

I hear another screech, and a car skids to a stop at our

window. Willie's wife, Renee, sticks her head out the window, her face flushed with rage. "Which of you girls said that?"

Laurel and I look at the floor, the ceiling, everywhere but at the irate woman. "Said what?" Laurel simpers in a phony, high-pitched voice.

"Oh no, you don't!" Mrs. Johnson floors it and skids around the corner of the building. Our day is about to get much, much worse.

Laurel takes a swallow of her drink. "I'm afraid we might be in a little trouble."

I take a deep breath to keep from shaking her. "*We* are not in trouble. But *you* are in mind-blowing, ten-on-the-Richter-scale trouble because—"

"Come on. It won't be that bad," she cuts me off and refills her cup with soda.

As Renee Johnson storms through the front door, my skin breaks out in goose pimples. "It's exponentially worse than you can imagine, Laurel. Because that woman you just propositioned is Willie's wife." Mrs. Johnson marches behind the counter and crashes into the back room with such force that her lacquered blond hair actually bounces. For Willie's sake, I hope he has both hands on the table.

Laurel chokes on her drink and breaks into a coughing fit. Soda spurts out her nose, which does nothing to help my semi-queasy stomach. I hand her a wad of paper napkins to mop her face.

Before she can catch her breath, Willie stomps out of the back with his angry wife on his heels. Until now, I've never seen a face that red without a second-degree sunburn. "Which of you said those things to my wife? No backtalk or excuses, just the truth. Right now!" His cheeks puff as the words explode from his mouth, and he seems on the verge of a heart attack.

Knowing Laurel, she's going to try to bluff her way out of trouble. "I saw Mrs. Johnson in the monitor, and I played a little joke on her." She smiles sheepishly. "I guess it wasn't such a good idea."

Willie's wife starts to speak, but Willie is way ahead of her. "Are you out of your mind? Making lewd remarks to a customer could ruin my business. This is a family restaurant!" Mrs. Johnson props her hands on her wide hips and glares at Laurel and me. In her bulging navy capris and overstuffed tank top, she looks like a wrestler waiting to attack.

Brad, a Cottonwood Creek freshman who's working the counter, has stopped to listen. For some unfathomable reason, he idolizes Willie. "Are you serious, dude? Because she does it, like, all the time."

Willie's eyes are the size of bowling balls. "How long has this been going on?"

Brad picks at a zit on his chin while he thinks. "A couple weeks at least. No. More like a month."

My stomach feels like I swallowed the smoothie mixer and it's stuck on high speed. It kicks into sonic mode when Willie turns on me. "Have you been saying those trashy things, too, Aspen?"

"Nah," Brad answers for me. "She keeps telling Lauren, Laura, whatever, to knock it off. But the bit—girl won't listen." He pops his gum. "Women. Whatcha gonna do?"

"I'm going to fire her, that's what." Willie is so pissed he can barely talk. "Laurel, turn in your hat and apron. You have five minutes to clean out your locker. If you're still here after that, I'm calling the cops."

Laurel's face is white with shock. I wonder if this is the first time she hasn't been able to talk her way out of trouble. She looks hopefully at me, but I clamp my lips together. If I lose this job, I'll be on house arrest until fall.

Willie taps his foot impatiently. "Well?"

"Fine, I'm going." Laurel rips off her hat and apron and drops them on the floor. "But you still owe me for last week." She turns on her heel and heads for the back room.

When I try to go after her, Willie blocks me. "You've been a good, reliable employee, Aspen. But if you don't get back to work immediately, I'll have to let you go, too."

I swallow hard before I answer. "Whatever you say, Willie. You're the boss."

He nods solemnly. "See that it stays that way."

fifteen

TUESDAY MORNING I PICK UP SAMMY STRIPERS AT MISS
Simmons's house to take him for our daily walk. I tried
to call Laurel last night after I got off work and twice this
morning, but she's not answering her cell. No doubt she's
pissed at me for not backing her up yesterday, but for once
I had to think of myself. Jobs in Cottonwood Creek are
scarce, and Mom and Dad expect me to buy most of my
own clothes. With Laurel gone, Willie will bump up my
hours again, which means more money but not much time
for myself. That's too bad because being under house arrest
is so enjoyable.

Clay is already getting out of his truck at the curb
when I see him. His chestnut hair is mussed, and his freckled nose and cheeks are sunburned. The way his white

T-shirt pulls tight across his muscled chest and shoulders sends little ripples up the back of my neck. "Hi, Aspen," he says, "mind if I walk with you?"

"Sure, that would be great." I can't imagine why he wants to see me again. At my last viewing, I was drunk and dripping like a soggy sheepdog. I won't allow myself to think about how revolting I smelled.

Clay lets Sammy sniff his hand before scratching him under the chin. Sammy half-closes his eyes and tilts his head back and forth to make sure Clay hits all the good spots. If I didn't like Sammy so much, I'd toss him out of the stroller and take his place. But the little black-and-white stinker has grown on me. I'm getting used to Miss Simmons, too. She's actually pretty funny if you don't take her crankiness seriously. It's been almost a week since she shook her walker at me, but I'm not ready to turn my back on her yet.

"So, Manny tells me you're grounded until your thirtieth birthday," Clay says as we fall into our side-by-side walking formation.

"If Mom had her way, she'd write the terms of my grounding into her last will and testament."

Clay chuckles. "Yeah, moms can be like that sometimes."

I try to concentrate on the conversation, but I keep noticing how awesome Clay's arm feels rubbing against me. "Was your mom strict when you were in high school?"

"Mom never grounded me, if that's what you mean, but I was too busy with school work and farming to get into trouble. When I was younger, she volunteered at school and with my 4-H group, so if I got out of line, she was always right there. Made it hard to be a delinquent." His blue eyes have tiny crinkles in the corners. "Every Labor Day our family hosts a barbecue at the farm for family and friends. If you're out on parole by then, you could meet her. That is, if you'd like to come."

Under no circumstances will I jump up and down and shriek. "Sounds like fun. Maybe—"

A rusted-out white truck pulls alongside us, and Buster hangs his flabby face out the window. "Hey, whatever Ass-wipe said, she's lying to you, dude!" Buster yells at volume ten, even though he's close enough for me to see the gross tobacco stains on his chin. "That baby ain't yours!"

"It's not Ass-face's, either." Ferret leans over. "She's so skinny it'd show if she got knocked up by a gnat! But no self-respecting gnat would go there."

"Ignore them," I tell Clay. "Those two have the collective mental capacity of a fruit fly." Then Kong's ginormous face rises from the back of the pickup, smooshed and red on the side where he was sleeping. "Oops, their mental capacity just plummeted to sub-amoebic levels."

Clay isn't in the mood to appreciate my humor. He's gone rigid from the hairline down. The way he's glowering at Buttferk would make me pee my pants. If I don't do something fast, I'm afraid he'll go after them. With three against one—two and a half, considering how wimpy Ferret is—Clay could get hurt.

"Shut up, morons! I'm babysitting." I step in front of the stroller to make sure they can't see Sammy. "You're scaring the baby."

"If your ugly face doesn't scare it, nothing will." Buster stuffs a wad of tobacco into his left cheek.

Clay covers the distance to the truck in three long strides. He grabs the front of Buster's grubby T-shirt and pulls the top half of his body out the window. Buster's eyes pop. He chokes, and chewing tobacco shoots out of his mouth.

"I disagree with the way you're talking to my friend," Clay says in a voice he might use to tell Buster the catfish are biting in the Raccoon River. "So the smart thing is for you to drive away now while I still have control of my temper. Got it?" Clay shakes Buster so that his head wobbles up and down. "Good. Now get out of here."

Kong bellows, "I don't think so!" and scales the side of the truck. Sadly, his shoelace snags in the crack between the tailgate and the truck bed. He halts abruptly in mid-leap and topples face-first onto the pavement.

Now that has to be humiliating.

I cover my mouth, but a chuckle sneaks out around the

edges. Buster is swearing and trying to break Clay's hold, but being half in and half out of the window limits his options. With his buddies temporarily disabled, Ferret is keeping a low profile in the passenger seat—literally. He's scrunched so low I can barely see the top of his head.

Clay looks over his shoulder at me. "Aspen, take Sammy and get out of here. I'll catch up with you later."

"Are you sure?" I hate to leave Clay with those three brutes, but he seems to have things under control. And they can't find out about Sammy. Who knows what awful things they'd do to him?

Clay motions me away with his head. "Yes. Now go!"

When I reach the corner, I stop behind a tall hedge and peek around it to see what's happening. Clay is holding Buster through the driver's window of the pickup while Kong climbs into the back. Kong sits down and hands his shoes to Clay. Then Buster slaps an object into Clay's open palm. One at a time, Clay tosses Kong's shoes into different parts of the lawn. Keeping an eye on the truck, Clay turns and heaves the object—Buster's truck key—into a trio of spiny bushes.

When Clay drives safely away in his pickup, I let my breath out. My legs are wobbling, but I push Sammy at warp speed to put as much distance as possible between Buttferk and me. I'm not that concerned about what those losers are going to do today. Buster and Kong are too lazy to come after me on foot, and Ferret is too much of a wimp. By the time Buster and Kong retrieve their stuff, Clay will be halfway home and I'll have Sammy safely back in Miss Simmons's house. But that only takes care of today—

"Hey, Aspen, are you all right?"

I yip and jump about a mile before I realize Clay has pulled his truck alongside me. Sammy goes on stink alert. "It's okay, Sammy. That's your good friend Clay. You like Clay." I stroke Sammy's back and talk softly until he lowers his tail.

"Sorry. I didn't mean to startle you," Clay says through the open window. "I couldn't leave without making sure you're okay."

I stop petting Sammy and check up and down the street. "I'm fine, but you need to get out of here before Buster and Kong come looking for you."

Clay chuckles. "They won't. Buster's busy looking for his ignition key in the bushes where he thinks I threw it."

"Didn't you? I saw—"

"Hey, you were supposed to be running away, not watching." He shakes his head at me. "What I threw was a rock I picked up off the street. I stuck Buster's truck key in an old envelope from my glove compartment, wrote his name on it, and dropped it in the mail collection box in front of the bank." Clay grins. "I'm sure Buster has a spare.

If not, the post office should get his key back to him by the end of the week."

"I'm impressed!" And in love. If it wouldn't scare Sammy, I'd dive through the open truck window onto Clay's lap.

"I was kind of proud of that one myself." Clay checks his rearview mirror. "Well, I'd better get to the golf course. We've had so much rain this summer that the grass is growing an inch a day." He shifts his truck into gear. "If those guys give you any more trouble, let me know."

I nod and wave as he drives away. It's reassuring to know that Buttferk is out of commission for the moment. But my sense of relief is temporary because it's only a matter of time before the Three Steaming Piles pool their evil energy and wreak revenge. Now they're not just going after Laurel and me. Clay has given them a brand-new target.

Laurel pouts for two more days before she finally answers my calls. Because we're both on house arrest, the best we can do is e-mail and message each other on Facebook and sneak in the occasional text or call on our cells. As part of my punishment Mom took away my laptop for three weeks. Until I get it back, I'm using the family room computer while my parents are at work.

Laurel's usually laid-back dad exploded when Willie

phoned and gave him the details about why she had been fired. Apparently it's bad business for the bank manager's daughter to be talking like a hooker, especially when her prospective clients might be bank customers, too. The good news—if there is any—is that Laurel's mom and her second family are hiking in Colorado until the second week of August. If it weren't for that, her dad would ship her off to Chicago in a heartbeat.

At the Sub Stop, Willie watches me like he's afraid I'll climb out the order window and give the customers a lap dance. He hasn't hired anyone to replace Laurel, so the rest of us are working extra shifts. Brad, the freshman who kind of saved my job, seems to think I owe him. Either he developed a serious coordination problem overnight or he's bumping into me on purpose. After it happened five times in one evening, I gently told him to back off or I'd push him into the deep-fat fryer. That seems to have taken care of the matter.

The day after Laurel and I start talking again, Sam and Tyler pull into the Sub Stop drive-through in Sam's yellow pickup. Sam's blond buzz cut is almost white from the sun, and his lips and nose are peeling. "Hey, Aspen, how's it going?" he says as they pull up to the window. Tyler leans forward and waves.

"Okay," I say with twice the enthusiasm I feel, which is none at all.

Sam hands me a wad of crumpled dollar bills. "Did

you and Laurel make a clean getaway after the party last weekend? We didn't see you when the cops rounded everyone up."

"Yes and no." I glance at the monitor to make sure no one is waiting to order. Willie is in the back room doing the end-of-June payroll, and I can hear him muttering and swearing through the closed door. "We escaped the raid but a cop picked us up on the road." I give Sam and Tyler a shortened version of the night's events while I pass their drinks and food through the window.

"You and Laurel got hauled into the police station! That is excellent!" Sam pumps his fist in the air. "All of us in the barn had to stand around while the cops called our parents and made them come and pick us up."

"Did the cop cuff you?" Tyler's chubby face is pink with excitement.

"Forget the cuffs," Sam says, licking his lips. "I want to know if you were strip-searched! Come on, give us some—"

I slide the window shut and walk away. Haven't I been punished enough?

I haven't heard from Clay since our brush with the Gruesome Threesome. Since he knows I'm in social quarantine, the best I can hope for is the two of us taking another stroll with Sammy. Miss Simmons is so happy with the way Sammy and I have bonded that she's mellowing out a little more every day. She hasn't turned into Mary Poppins, but I've stopped sniffing her cookies and lemonade to check for poison. Most days we sit on her front porch for a few minutes after I've walked Sammy. Miss Simmons tells me about her younger sister who lives with her husband in Vermont and her favorite niece who calls every Sunday. Of course, her number-one topic is the people who get on her nerves, who seem to be at least half the population of Cottonwood Creek. I listen and nod and make appropriate comments. It seems to work for both of us.

The real beneficiary of my punishment is Carmine. Since I'm willing to do almost anything to escape the house, he gets treated to several walks a day. He'd gotten chubby after a winter of lying around the house, but all the exercise has whipped him into shape. By running behind him, I'm getting into shape by default.

But having a skunk, a dog, and a semi-cranky old lady as best friends isn't what I had planned for my summer.

Late Friday night I'm enjoying an R-rated dream starring Clay and me when "Sweet Home Alabama" jars me awake. For the past week I've slept with my cell phone on my pillow at night—just in case Clay decides to call. I've practiced my sexy hello, and it comes out perfect. Until tonight, all that's come of my preparations is a rectangular imprint on my left cheek.

"I have to get out of this house!" Laurel howls. "I haven't seen another living person for days!" She's been texting me all day, each one more frantic than the last.

I say good-bye to R-rated Clay and stack the pillows behind my head. "What about your dad?"

"I said a *living* person. My father doesn't qualify." Laurel groans dramatically. "Please, Aspen, I have to see you. I'm losing my sanity."

Wisely, I refrain from commenting. "Sorry. I'm getting time off for good behavior, but I still can't come over for another week. And that's only if it's okay with your dad."

"A week? No way!" She's working herself into a hysterical frenzy. "The walls are closing in on me! If I don't get out of here tonight, I'll go insane!"

"Come on, Laurel. You can get through this." I haven't used my "talking down from the roof" voice for a while, and it's a little rusty. "Take long, deep breaths, drink some warm milk—"

"Nooooo! I can't! Please . . ." Everything else she's saying drowns in sobs. After a long minute, she recovers her voice. "Please, please, please, Aspen," she says between hiccups, "meet me in the park by the swings. We can swing and talk and pretend we're little kids again. Please."

Laurel goes on like that for another ten minutes before I finally give in. Sneaking out is the stupidest thing I could possibly do. But Laurel is in genuine pain. As her best friend, it's my obligation to help her through this.

There's no sense trying to make Carmine stay home, so I don't even try. We slip out the back door and through the gate into the alley behind our house. The sultry air leaves a coating of dampness on my skin. It's hard to believe it's already the second of July. If I get away with tonight's escapade, maybe Clay and I will watch the Fourth of July fireworks together Sunday night. All I have to do is talk Manny into bringing him over.

The park is halfway between my house and Laurel's, so it's easier to walk than drag out my bike. Flags hang limply from streetlight poles and most front porches. Mailbox planters overflow with geraniums, petunias, and out-of-control sweet potato vines. Fireflies dance over the freshly cut lawns to a chorus of serenading cicadas. The cicadas make me think of one summer years ago when I collected dried cicada skins and used them as invading aliens in skits with my dolls. I don't think Laurel would have been excited about playing with me back then.

Carmine bounds ahead of me, smelling for any new pee-mail deposits and making his own contributions. That dog has a bladder the size of a basketball.

Carmine and I walk on the asphalt driveway past the soccer fields, volleyball and tennis courts, and the Frisbee golf course. The driveway will lead us to the pavilion and picnic area just west of the playground. Beyond that, it connects to a jogging/biking trail that circles the park, continues past the business district, and joins the Raccoon River Valley Trail on the other side of town. The entire park is only about two blocks long, but it's the social center of Cottonwood Creek for picnics, family reunions, and little kids' play dates. The only teens you'll see here during the day are those playing sports, but I've heard the shadowy areas by the creek see plenty of action at night.

The park closes at ten thirty, but the city keeps the streetlights by the pavilion on all night to discourage vandalism. Which makes me wonder why they're not on tonight. The only light I see comes from the crescent moon. Although I'm a little creeped out by the darkness, Laurel is counting on me to show up. Besides, I have Carmine to warn me if some pervert is waiting to spring.

Because it's so dark, I can't see Laurel until I'm a few feet away. She's slouched on the wooden seat, listlessly swinging back and forth.

"Hey!" I whisper as I approach. "Your human and canine reinforcements are here."

"You came!" Laurel steps out of the swing and hugs me fiercely. "I knew you would." Her voice is muffled against my shoulder.

While we're hugging, Carmine takes the opportunity to stick his nose up her rear. "Carmine, you haven't changed a bit in the last two weeks!" She laughs and pushes him away.

Laurel lets me go, and we drop into adjacent swings. "You have no idea how glad I am to see you—and your perverted dog." Carmine licks her bare knee, and she rubs his neck. "He's given me the most action I've seen all summer."

I swing a little to stir up a breeze. "Feeling better now?"

She leans back in the swing and looks up at the stars. "I am. I never realized how small our house is. My claustrophobia kicked into high gear."

"Is your dad speaking to you yet?" I pump my legs harder, loving the way the wind feels on my face. Laurel starts swinging, too.

"Barely. He—"

A muffled explosion cuts into Laurel's words. Two more louder and closer blasts follow the first. Carmine's ears flatten. He lets out an unearthly squeal and tears in the opposite direction with his tail plastered against his rump.

More explosions come one after the other—some echo as if they're going off inside a cave, some are deafening. I bail out of my swing with Laurel close behind.

"What is that?" she gasps.

"Probably fireworks," I say, although the blasts seem too loud for firecrackers. "Or someone is using the pavilion for target practice. We need to go." I start walking back the way I came.

"Wait!" Laurel says, catching up to me. "Shouldn't we see what's going on?"

I keep walking. "No, we should not. We're not even supposed to be out here. Remember?" Three more explosions reinforce my decision.

Laurel clutches the sleeve of my T-shirt. "But you said it might be target practice. What if someone's shooting at animals?"

My steps get slower.

"Suppose they found a nest of bunnies and they're killing them one at a time?" Her eyes are round with horror. "Or they're wounding them and watching them suffer."

I know guys who are that perverse. "Okay, but we have to be really careful."

This section of the park is mostly open space, so there's not much cover for us. We slip from tree to tree, hiding in the meager shadows. My muscles tense as if I'm expecting a bullet to hit me between the shoulder blades.

"Let's get behind that." Laurel points at a tall metal trash can across the driveway from the pavilion. It seems like as good a place to hide as any, and we dash toward it.

"Hey, Buster! Somebody's over there!"

Laurel and I duck behind the trash can, but it's too late. If I had two brain cells to rub together, I'd have known in a nanosecond who was making all the noise in the park.

But a person with two brain cells would be home in bed, not cringing behind a smelly, overflowing garbage can.

"Come out, come out, whoever you are!" Ferret calls in a creepy singsong voice.

Just like that, my bladder is bursting. And squatting here is putting pressure in a very uncomfortable place.

"Save your breath, Ferret," Buster tells him. "I'll flush the rats out of their hole."

A small, round object lands on top of the garbage can. It's too late to run, so I squeeze my eyes shut and clap my hands over my ears. Everything happens at once. There's an ear-shattering explosion. The metal can trembles. Shredded trash rains on my head.

And a police siren screams in the distance.

Laurel and I exchange looks of horror, but neither of us moves from our hiding place. I feel like the opossum Carmine cornered in the backyard last summer, except playing dead won't make Buttferk give up and leave us alone.

"Haven't had enough?" Buster yells. "There's plenty more where that one came from!"

Three golf-ball-size firecrackers plop at our feet. Laurel and I break cover and sprint for the closest tree. When the M-80s detonate with cracks like rifle fire, Laurel's mouth opens as wide as a bear trap. I'm almost positive she's screaming, but my ears have gone numb.

More M-80s shower around us. I cringe and cover my

ears, but nothing happens. Then I see that their fuses aren't sparking. Why are those dimwits tossing unlit firecrackers?

Buster, Ferret, and Kong jump into Buster's pickup. He guns the engine and pulls a sharp U-turn in the driveway. The truck screeches to a stop in front of us. Buster and Kong leap out. Before Laurel and I can run, they back us against the tree we've been using for cover. My bladder almost lets go when I see a thick chain dangling from Buster's right hand. Kong is passing a tire iron from one giant paw to the other.

"What is it with you two bitches? Every time I turn around you're messing in my business," Buster snarls in my face. "Now you call the cops on us for having a little fun." My ears are buzzing, but at this distance I don't miss a word.

"W-We didn't." Laurel's voice breaks. "We were just—"

"Shut up!" Buster grabs her shoulders and shakes her like a damp towel. The chain he's holding slaps against her leg. "When the cops get here, you're going to say you was shooting off them M-80s."

"We was never here," Kong says in case Laurel and I couldn't figure out what Buster meant. Kong slams the tire iron against the tree trunk so hard I feel it tremble.

"Because if we even think you've ratted us out, no fancy home alarm system is gonna protect you." Buster bares his snaggy brown teeth at Laurel. "Understand?"

Laurel's head bobs up and down, and she looks like she's

going to throw up. She was hoping her Facebook post about their new home security system would scare Buster off.

"You"—Buster pulls the chain tight between his fists and holds it in front of my throat—"and your smart-ass boyfriend will get double whatever she gets."

"Don't forget her asshole brother," Kong adds helpfully.

Buster's lip curls in a malicious smirk that makes me feel like cockroaches are crawling under my skin. "Oh, I won't."

Now the police siren sounds like it's coming from the next block. Buster moves in on me. I smash my body against the tree to prevent body contact. "Remember what I'm saying, Tree Scabs." He cuts a look at Laurel so she won't feel left out. "One word from either of you, and people will get messed up real bad." He cracks the chain against the ground for emphasis.

"Come on. Let's hit it." Buster signals Kong, and they both swagger to the pickup. Buster slides behind the wheel while Kong vaults into the truck bed.

My leg muscles turn to pudding, and I slide down the trunk to the ground. The buzzing in my ears seems to get louder. Buster guns his engine and swerves the truck so close that gravel showers my legs.

Ferret, who's always bravest when he's running away, leans out the passenger window and yells, "Beep your house hut, switches!" as they speed off.

Laurel gives me a hand up. I test my shaky legs, which haven't decided what they want to do. "What did he say?" My voice sounds hollow.

She puts her mouth to my ear, which is buzzing like a swarm of bees. "He said, 'Keep your mouths shut, bitches.'"

"We were never here, so what's to talk about?" My legs have steadied enough to support my weight. "Let's get out of here before the police arrive. The smartest thing to do is stay off the streets."

But Laurel is gathering up the unexploded M-80s and stuffing them in her shorts pockets.

"What are you doing? Leave those here and let's get—"

A police patrol car pulls up to the pavilion with its lights flashing and its spotlight sweeping the area. I squat behind my new tree friend where Laurel is scooping up illegal explosives, but it's hopeless. The light trains on us and sticks.

Déjà vu really sucks.

I shade my eyes from the glare with my right hand and stand up. Mom is going to go up like a Roman candle when she hears about this.

An officer steps out of the car and starts toward us. The glare makes it impossible to see details, but his size and shape are horribly familiar.

"You're not going to say anything, right?" Laurel is talking from the side of her mouth like a gangster. "If we tell, they're going to do something really awful to us. Or our families."

I shiver. When Buster held that chain up to my throat, I thought he was going to strangle me. He already hates Laurel and me, and he hates Clay for making him look like a fool at Miss Simmons's house. Buster is looking for an excuse to take revenge, and Kong and Ferret will be happy to tag along. I can see Buttferk ambushing Clay or Manny in an isolated spot where it would be three against one. And what about Ferret's threat to slash more than our tires? If those goons hurt people I care about because of me, I'll never forgive myself.

Officer Sierra throws his hands in the air. "You have got to be kidding me! I was sure you'd be grounded until the Second Coming."

Laurel's voice has suddenly gone missing, so I have to answer. "Well, we sort of are . . . grounded. But Laur—we were feeling really, really cooped up. So we walked over here to swing and get some fresh air."

Officer Sierra looks at the fragments around us. "And how do these illegal fireworks fit in?"

"Well . . . uh—"

Laurel jabs her elbow just below my left boob. "Those were my idea. You know, Fourth of July, firecrackers? The perfect combination for a little harmless fun."

"Except in Iowa, fireworks are illegal." He holds out his

hand and Laurel hands over one of the unlit firecrackers. "And these M-80s aren't legal anywhere—at least, nowhere in the Midwest. So I'm interested to know where you got your hands on them."

Me too. I glance at Laurel.

"Sorry. I can't reveal my source." Laurel lifts her chin. "Supplier/client privilege."

Officer Sierra snorts. "There is no supplier/client privilege. What's the story? Did your boyfriend buy the fireworks for you?"

I choke back a laugh, which starts a coughing fit. He waits until I catch my breath, then he pounces. "Okay, Aspen, you tell me. Where did you girls get them?"

His eyes and Laurel's bore into me as I bite on my lower lip, trying to decide what to do. The way Buster and Kong scared the crap out of me just now, I'd love to tell Officer Sierra and let him handle them. On the other hand, he's caught Laurel and me lying twice *and* I've puked on his shoes, but he still hasn't thrown us in jail. I'd rather take my chances with the law than have Buttferk stomp us into dust. "They just kind of fell out of the sky."

Officer Sierra massages his forehead. "All right, then. You know how this goes." When my parents hear about this little adventure, they're going to lock me up and flush the key.

He marches us to the squad car and opens the back

189

door. Before we get in, he makes us empty our pockets and puts the rest of the M-80s into a plastic bag. Once we're locked in and he's in the driver's seat, he says, "Bright and early tomorrow morning, I'll be back out here to see if you girls did any damage with your 'harmless fun.'"

He turns around and puts the car into gear. "If I find *any* damage at all, I guarantee that you girls will personally make restitution. That's in addition to any monetary fines you'll be required to pay. Depending on the judge's mood, those can be anywhere from one hundred to two hundred fifty dollars."

Laurel and I gulp in unison.

This is without question the worst summer of my entire life.

sixteen

"THIS IS THE MOST DISGUSTING THING I'VE EVER DONE. THESE portable potties are grosser than pig poop," Laurel whines through the scarf wrapped over her nose and mouth. "I swear I'm going to puke." She swipes at the flies swarming around her face and hair, but it's pointless when we're outnumbered a million to two.

I dip my sponge into the bucket of disinfectant and water sitting outside the portable toilet. My gloves are industrial-strength rubber and reach almost to my elbows, but the infested water slops over the top and drips inside. "You've said that at least ten times. Just throw up and get it over with!"

Laurel's lucky that I haven't dumped a bucket of slop

over her head. Because of her I'm spending my Saturday scrubbing crap from the portable toilets in the park instead of doing my shift at the Sub Stop. Saturday of the Fourth of July weekend is our busiest day of the summer, and Willie was monstrously pissed when I called this morning to bail on him. I hope I still have a job on Monday.

I suppose we're lucky that creating volcanic human waste in portable potties is the worst damage Buttferk did with their fireworks last night. Too bad the Parks Commission brought in ten extra toilets for the Fourth of July celebration. And Buster, Kong, and Ferret dropped M-80s into every one of them.

If I were in a thankful mood, I'd say that at least we're scrubbing the toilets before several thousand people use them to relieve themselves of their Independence Day hot dogs, corn on the cob, and beer. But my mood is not thankful.

It was nothing short of pathetic at twelve forty-five this morning when Laurel and I took our usual places on the wooden bench at the Cottonwood Creek Police Department. What kind of lowlife has a "usual place" in a police station? I was furious at Laurel for dragging me into another mess, but almost as pissed at myself for letting her. So I sat boiling mad on the hard bench and kept my mouth shut.

This time Laurel's dad didn't look the least bit sleepy when he marched in to get her. He was wearing a tan polo shirt neatly tucked into pressed khakis. His hair was slicked into place. But his jaw could have been made of cement, and he wouldn't even look at Laurel. When Officer Sierra spelled out the details of our latest crime, Mr. Piedmont's face turned from red to white and back again. Instead of taking Laurel home after Officer Sierra finished talking, he leaned against the wall and tapped his shiny loafers on the floor until my dad showed up.

By contrast, my dad seemed almost pleasant, but I wasn't fooled. The madder he is, the quieter he gets. And Mom's staying at home was a very bad sign. It meant she was too pissed to trust herself in public. Putting those two factors together spelled disaster for me.

After my dad selected a place on the wall beside Mr. Piedmont, Officer Sierra went over the specifics of our vandalism one more time. I guess he didn't want our dads to miss any of the juicy details. While he talked, he paced back and forth with his hands locked behind his back. Since I'd already heard more than I wanted, I tuned out Officer Sierra's voice and focused on more pleasant topics, like how I could survive living on the streets.

"—so I'll assess the situation at the park as soon as the sun comes up," Officer Sierra was saying when I tuned back in. "After I see where things stand, I'd like your permission to put the girls to work in repairing any damage they caused."

Laurel's dad answered first, biting off his words through gritted teeth. "Whatever consequences you decide for Laurel are fine with me, Officer Sierra. The tougher the better. She deserves anything and everything you dish out."

Not to be outdone, Dad jumped in. "Mrs. Parks and I want you to be as hard on Aspen as you think is necessary. She will also receive consequences at home." The tight control in his voice made my stomach seize up. I was so panicked that I almost gave in and told what really happened. But I'd kept quiet too long. It would sound like I was lying to avoid being punished.

Officer Sierra let us go home about one fifteen. After a silent car ride, Dad went straight to bed and left me standing in the kitchen. I waited, expecting Mom to rush downstairs and blow up at me. But the only thing I heard was my heart pounding. After about twenty minutes of bracing for the worst, I drank a glass of milk and went to bed. I could have saved myself the trouble of undressing because I didn't have a prayer of falling asleep. At least Carmine was glad to see me. He licked my sweaty knee a few times, plopped his head across my shins, and snored with happiness.

I was still awake when Officer Sierra called at four thirty a.m. to give Mom and Dad his park damage report. He picked me up at five thirty, and we swung by Laurel's house, where she and her dad were waiting out front. It's just after noon now, and I'm ready to drop. Thank God this is our last toilet.

Laurel and I step out to let Officer Sierra do his inspection. He looks around and says, "Good enough. Like you did with the other ones, leave the door propped open until it dries out."

Laurel rips the scarf from her face and drags in a huge gulp of air. "Hallelujah! I can breathe again!"

We tug our gloves off and drop them on the ground. My fingers are white and pruney. Until I've scrubbed my hands with bleach and three kinds of soap, they're not coming anywhere near my face.

"Wait a minute, girls," Officer Sierra says. His face is shadowed with stubble, and the circles under his brown eyes look like bruises. "Don't take those gloves off yet."

"Why not?" Laurel uses her forearm to brush back her hair. She's not taking any chances with her hands, either. "We've cleaned every one of those reeking portable potties."

Officer Sierra scans the line of outdoor toilets by the park shelter. "So you have." An unpleasant smile turns up the corners of his mouth. "And, after you pick up all the firecracker debris, you should be done for today."

I look at the thousands of red paper scraps littering the road, the grass, and the trail. My breath comes out as a groan.

Officer Sierra's grin gets broader. "Hey, no problem, girls. Just think of it as the continuing saga of your harmless fun."

I thought Officer Sierra would at least give us the stick things with the pointed ends to skewer the miniscule M-80 pieces. No such luck. We have to bend over, pick them up one by one, and drop them into trash bags.

I'm hot and miserable, and I smell worse than the toilets. My thighs and back are screaming in pain. My stomach is growling. And Laurel is the last person in the universe I want to talk to.

"Hey, look at the bright side." I know she wants me to ask what she means, but the only bright side I see involves her lingering and painful death. "We're going to be in next week's *Cottonwood Creek Gazette*. You know, where they list the police calls. That's going to get us noticed."

"And you think that would be a good thing? Your dad will be twice as furious if his bank's clients see your name in the paper." It doesn't seem possible for my mom to be madder than she already is, but I'm sure she'll do her best. "In what universe is public humiliation something to celebrate?"

I fling a handful of M-80 guts into my trash bag.

"I'm not even allowed to watch the stupid Fourth of July parade tomorrow!" The fury I've been holding back explodes. "Thanks to you, my parents are threatening to handcuff me to my bed at night! Thanks to you, I've lost my shot at the one guy who's ever been interested in me! Thanks to you, Laurel, my life is ruined!"

The trash bag slips from Laurel's grasp. She slides to the ground like a melting ice cream cone and buries her face in her filthy gloves. Her tanned shoulders shake with sobs.

I grind my teeth together, steeling myself. Knowing Laurel, she's putting on a show to get my sympathy. Too bad I'm fresh out. I turn my back on her and scoop up some more firecracker parts.

Laurel deserves to be yelled at after everything she's put me through. All I wanted was a calm, relaxing summer. If anyone should have a good cry, it's me.

She earned everything I said to her, and more. I hope she cries so hard her eyeballs swell up like water balloons. Taking a stranglehold on the neck of my garbage bag, I drag it to the other end of the park. This time I'm not going to apologize. No way, no how.

When Laurel realizes she's not going to get any sympathy, her bawling drops a notch or two. From the corner of my eye I watch as she gets to her feet and goes back to picking up trash. She keeps glancing toward me, but I don't let her catch me watching her.

Two hours pass in stony silence while we clean up the park, piece by tedious piece. My anger carries me for the first hour or so. After that I'm too numb to think or feel.

Eventually the heat and stench of my own sweat make me dizzy. I dump my bag on the ground and stagger over to the bottles of water that Officer Sierra has kindly left for us in the shade. The water temperature is somewhere between lukewarm and hot, but it takes the edge off my dizziness. After several swallows I feel almost subhuman again.

"I'm sorry, Aspen," Laurel says from behind me, causing me to slop water down my sweat-soaked T-shirt. "Everything is my fault. You wouldn't have been in any of this trouble if I hadn't dragged you into it." She wipes her nose on the filthy tail of her T-shirt. "I understand if you don't want to be my friend anymore."

I clench and unclench my jaw. "I'm definitely pissed at you. . . ." By rights I should make her suffer for a few days—or weeks—but I've never been good at staying mad. "But we're still friends."

"Oh, thank you! Thank you!" Laurel throws her arms around my waist, and our two sticky bodies connect with a wet splat. We pull apart, and our T-shirts stay stuck together for a second.

"OMG!" Laurel's lips curl away from her teeth. "That was the grossest hug ever!"

I turn my lips up in what might be a smile. At this point, it's hard to tell. "Crap, puke, and sweat have kind of been this summer's buzzwords. But they're all behind us now."

"No, they're not!" Laurel's eyes fill with tears. "Dad's going to make me work at a chicken farm!"

That sits me back on my heels. "What?"

"Dad was really pissed when I lost my job at the Sub Stop. He told me to find another job or he'd find one for me." Laurel splashes some bottled water on her face. "I figured he'd get over it, like always, so I blew it off. But on the way home from the police station last night or this morning, whenever it was, he said he got me a job at the EggstraGood Chicken Farm for the rest of the summer." Laurel drags her scarf out of her pocket and blows her nose with a honk. "It's horrible! Dirty, smelly, stupid chickens and their dirty, smelly chicken poop."

I pat her shoulder. "Hey, chickens aren't so bad. When I was in third grade our class hatched out some baby chicks, and they were adorable."

"Those were fluffy little chicks." Laurel blows her nose again. "I'll be up to my butt in big, ugly, stupid chickens."

"Granted, chickens aren't known for their high IQs, but they're not that ugly. And, they're kind of funny to watch. Remember that YouTube video of the rooster chasing the Rottweiler around the yard?"

Laurel smiles a little. "Yeah. That was pretty hilarious."

"And EggstraGood is a free-range farm, so you'll get

to be outdoors all day. That's way better than being on house arrest." The more we talk about it, the better it sounds to me.

"Really? Maybe you're right." She wipes her eyes. "Chickens are animals, after all, and I love animals."

The little warning bell tinkles in the back of my head. "Just remember that chickens end up being chicken sandwiches. So don't get too attached to them."

Laurel dismisses that with a wave. "Who could possibly get attached to a chicken?"

seventeen

WHEN I COME TO WORK ON MONDAY AFTER THE FOURTH OF July, Willie treats me to a soul-stirring lecture about the American work ethic and assigns me to perpetual deep-fat-fryer duty, but he doesn't fire me. I'd like to think it's because I'm such a valuable employee. More likely, he's keeping me on because most high school kids aren't looking for work in July. By the time he got a new person trained, it would be time for him or her to go back to school.

The next two weeks drag by. My parents have me under twenty-four-hour surveillance, which means my life consists of the Sub Stop, Sammy, and the ten thousand chores Mom and Dad dream up for me. According to Mom, working me to the bone will ensure that I'm too tired to get into trouble. What she doesn't say is that she and Dad derive sadistic pleasure from watching me suffer.

Once or twice I mention Clay to Manny, but he just shakes his head. No wonder. Clay has probably written me off as a criminal in the making. At least Carmine hasn't deserted me. At home he sticks to me like a burr, so every time I turn around I trip over him. For the past week or so, he hasn't wanted to go for our walks. When I take him out, he plants his butt on the sidewalk and whines until I let him back into the house. He seems to be limping a little, too, and I wonder if he's getting arthritis. If he's not better soon, I'm going to ask Mom if we can take him to the vet.

Despite Laurel's prediction, our names don't even make it into the paper. Since neither of us is eighteen yet, we're listed as "two juvenile females, age seventeen" even though my birthday isn't until next week. So much for notoriety.

That doesn't mean we're forgotten. Every day when I'm biking to or from work, one or more of the Buttferk gang just "happens" to be driving by. Whatever piece of crap they're driving slows to a crawl, then they stick their ugly heads out the windows and snarl. I do my best to be cool and ignore them, but I feel like fire ants are running over my skin. They never say anything, which is even creepier because I don't know what's on their evil minds.

The only time I see Laurel is when we have to appear in court on the fireworks charges. We meet in a small courtroom that's nothing like what I've seen on TV. Judge Boris—according to the little sign in the holder by the door—is sitting at a small, elevated wooden desk shuffling through a sheaf of papers. She's wearing a black robe just like TV judges do, with a white collar sticking out the top. Her hair is chin-length, brown, and curly, and black-rimmed glasses hang off the end of her nose. From the little I can see of her body, she's on the thin side, but not super-thin. She looks a lot like my fourth-grade teacher, only with frown lines where her laugh lines should be. Laurel and I are seated with our parents in the gallery, which consists of two rows of folding chairs lined up against the wall.

My heart kicks against my ribs like a wild stallion. Sweat pours down my sides, and I'm afraid I'll pee myself if I uncross my legs. Officer Sierra said we'd have to pay fines, but what if the judge has a surprise for us—like time at juvenile hall?

It took some pleading from Laurel and me, but our parents graciously permitted the prisoners to sit side by side. Laurel leans into my ear and whispers, "You were right about the chicken farm. Chickens are kind of funny and cute—and so is the owner's son, Steve. Working there is the best thing that's happened to me all summer."

Well, isn't that lovely for her? Maybe Steve and the chickens will bring us an omelet while we're in jail.

"And that's not the best part," she continues. "Dad got tired of driving me all the way out to EggstraGood, so he bought me a car."

"A car!" I practically shout. Next she'll say her dad's letting her move into her own apartment to be closer to the fowl.

Mom frowns and shushes me, but it's too late. Judge Boris has stopped shuffling her papers. She'll probably give me extra jail time for contempt of court.

The judge asks Laurel and me to stand up and approach the bench, which is the only TV-like thing that's happened so far. My leg muscles are quivery, but somehow I wobble over. It does me good to see that Laurel's a little shaky, too.

When Judge Boris asks for my plea, my mouth sticks shut. Every fiber of my body wants to scream, "Innocent, innocent, innocent!" But with Buttferk stalking me, I can't risk it. So I mutter, "Guilty" in a strangled voice and prepare to take my punishment.

The judge removes her reading glasses and peers at us. "Officer Sierra isn't able to testify today, but he submitted a written statement concerning your case."

Laurel's gulp is so loud that Judge Boris quirks an eyebrow at her. I clench my pelvic muscles and pray the wetness on my inner thighs is sweat.

"Since he is the officer of record—and seems to know you young women quite well—I've chosen to follow his recommendations."

If I do whatever the prison guards tell me and avoid all the women with neck tattoos, I might—

"Therefore, each of you is fined fifty dollars plus court costs. And, per Officer Sierra's proposal, you'll serve six months unsupervised probation." Judge Boris looks down on us from on high. "The next time you see Officer Sierra—which had better not be in his official capacity—you should thank him for requesting leniency."

"We will, Your Honor. Thank you, Your Honor," Laurel and I babble.

Before we leave, I write a check for $157 to the Clerk of Court—apparently courts don't come cheap—and say good-bye to Laurel.

While our parents are talking in the corner, she says, "See, everything worked out okay after all."

"You mean it worked out okay for you. You ended up with a fun job, a cute guy, and a car." I shove my checkbook into my purse. "My only source of excitement is betting the other workers at the Sub Stop how often Willie's wife will drop in to make sure he's not boinking the help."

Two days later, my life—which is already in complete shambles—takes a turn for the worse.

Now that Willie thinks he's whipped me back into shape, he's allowing me to man the drive-through window again. To make sure I don't have time to get into trouble, he has me doing both jobs—taking orders and delivering the food. During the lunch and dinner rush it gets so busy that I'm talking to people at the menu board and the window at the same time. But working the drive-through is better than standing over the deep-fat fryer, so I'm keeping my mouth shut for the next five weeks. Besides, when I'm swamped with work, time goes faster, and this summer can't end soon enough for me.

This morning Willie has already retreated to the back room. Since business is even slower than usual, I'm leaning on the window ledge, daydreaming. Clay and I are having a picnic on a grassy bank of Cottonwood Creek. He gazes adoringly at me while dappled sunshine filters through the leaves—no mosquitoes, floating trash, or swampy creek smell. Our hands clasp and his head inclines toward mine. I close my eyes in anticipation of his kiss—

"Hey, Ass-wipe! Are you puckering up to kiss the boss's ass?"

Daydream to nightmare in two seconds. That has to be a record.

I open my eyes to see Ferret's pointed snout poking out his car window. He's grown a soul patch, which nicely complements his dangling nose hairs. Someone should braid them together and shut his mouth permanently. Buster and Kong are mercifully absent.

"If you want to order something, you have to drive around to the order screen." Without the other two-thirds of Buttferk to back him up, Ferret is more creepy than intimidating. "If you don't want to order, you'll have to leave."

"I hear you and Low-rent had the good sense to keep your mouths shut in court the other day." Ferret's eyes shift from left to right like he's a covert operative for the CIA. "See that it stays that way."

"Listen, *Ferret*." I put extra emphasis on the nickname he hates. "Laurel and I didn't say anything—this time. But if you keep following and threatening me, I'll be happy to change my mind."

"Is that so?" He rubs his index finger across the caterpillar hanging under his lip. "On another topic, me and the guys are wondering what you push around in that buggy every morning. It sure ain't a baby."

My mouth goes dry. "Of course it is. I babysit for my neighbor."

"Yeah? Well, we've been watching you—and that dried-up, crippled old hag. She ain't raising no baby. No way, no how."

They've been watching Miss Simmons, too! What do they want with her? "Get your head screwed on straight, Ferret. What else would I be doing?"

"That's what we've been wondering." He nods sagely. "But it's a known fact that old hags hoard valuable stuff—money, jewelry, antiques, all that crap."

An uneasy feeling settles in my stomach. "Now I know you're insane! Miss Simmons is a poor, lonely old lady who's recovering from a hip replacement." A stroke of genius hits me. "Since you have to know, she owns one of those super lifelike dolls they sell on the Internet. The poor old thing treats it just like a baby, including taking it for a daily stroll. I'm pushing it around until her hip heals."

Feeling triumphant, I add, "It's a big stroller, Ferret. If you want, I can squeeze your dolly in, too."

"By the way, Ass-face, it's a bad idea to let your mangy dog run loose." He guns the engine of his junky car. "Next time he annoys somebody, they might shoot him with a shotgun instead of a pellet gun."

Ferret's lips pull back in an ugly smile. "And if you change your mind about shooting your mouth off, your mutt could end up under the wheels of somebody's car."

As Ferret's piece-of-crap car squeals away, all I can do is stare in horror. Carmine never hurt anyone, and one of those three psychos shot him. What would they do to someone they hate?

eighteen

AS SOON AS FERRET LEAVES, I CALL MOM AND BEG HER TO TAKE Carmine to the vet. First I tell her about his limping and being scared to go outdoors. I cap it off by saying a guy was bragging at the Sub Stop about shooting dogs from his car with a pellet gun. Of course she wants to know the guy's name, but I insist I've never seen him before.

I'd love to have Buttferk locked away for the rest of their unnatural lives. But, even with solid proof against them, nobody gets life in prison for wounding a dog. As long as the three of them are in Cottonwood Creek, poor Carmine isn't safe.

Two hours later, Mom calls me on my cell. "You were right, Aspen. Dr. Riordan took X-rays and found three pellets in Carmine's flank. Luckily the pellets were just under the skin, so he was able to give Carmine a local anesthetic and pull them out."

The black cloud over my head gets lighter. "So he's going to be okay?"

"Carmine should be fine. Dr. Riordan said if he had been shot at close range, the pellets might have done serious muscle damage."

Fear and anger rumble in my stomach. When those goons hurt my family, they went too far.

I hear Carmine's excited bark on the other end of the phone. "Here's a treat for you, Carmine, for being such a good boy at the doctor," Mom croons.

Picturing Carmine's grin as he wolfs down his favorite biscuits makes me smile.

"Aspen, if that maniac comes into the restaurant again, you get his name or license number for the police. Until he's caught, Carmine will have to be tied up whenever he's outdoors. We can't trust him not to climb the fence."

Thanks to those three jackasses, Carmine and I are both under house arrest.

After Mom and Dad have gone to bed, I call Laurel. She answers her phone in a whisper. "Hold on, Aspen. Let me see what Dad's doing."

While I wait for her to come back on the line, I sit up

and scratch Carmine's ears. He is lying across the foot of my bed with his head resting on my legs. Whenever I look at the bare patch where the vet shaved him, I want to hit somebody. The three pellet wounds are red slashes in his pale skin.

"It's okay," she says in her normal voice. "He's watching some sports program on TV. As long as the reception is okay, he won't notice if the house caves in around him." The rustling in the background tells me she's getting comfortable. "So, what's up?"

"Buster, Ferret, and Kong are infected boils on the ass of humanity."

She snorts. "Tell me something I don't already know."

I repeat Ferret's threats in as much detail as I can remember. In the past I've dismissed him as nothing but mouth, but the holes in Carmine's side won't let me do that anymore. No matter which one of them pulled the trigger, the three of them shot my dog.

Laurel's outrage crackles through my phone. "I can't believe they shot Carmine! Anyone who hurts an animal is the lowest, scummiest piece of crap on earth! If one of them hurt Cleo, I'd cut off his balls and use them for Hacky Sacks."

"Laurel, that is the grossest thing I've ever heard . . . and an excellent idea. Wait—who's Cleo?"

"She's my new BFF. We bonded instantly." I can actually hear her smiling.

I feel like I've been punched in the stomach. "What? I'm trapped in the nightmare hell of the worst summer on record, and now you have a new best friend?"

"Not a human best friend," she says in a soothing voice. "A best friend like Carmine."

Relief mixes with confusion. "You got a dog? I thought your whole family is allergic."

"She isn't a dog, and I don't exactly have her. Not yet, anyway." Laurel pauses mysteriously. "Cleo is a chicken."

My legs jerk. "An EggstraGood Chicken Farm chicken?" Carmine raises his head and looks at me. Then he lies back down with a sigh.

"Yes, and she's so adorable!" Laurel gushes. "She comes running to me every morning the second I walk into the chicken yard, and she makes the cutest little cluck-ing sounds."

"Don't all the chickens do that?"

"Well, sort of." There's a pause while Laurel thinks that over. "But Cleo follows me absolutely everywhere. She likes it when I scratch her between the wings, and she loves to be carried."

There is no way for this to end well. "Laurel . . . honey," I say gently, "you know what those chickens are raised for, don't you?"

"Don't worry, Aspen. These are egg-laying chickens, not chickens for eating. I asked that question the very first day."

I bet she still leaves carrots for the Easter Bunny. "But what happens when they stop laying?"

"They're put out to pasture, I guess. You know, like that farmer will do with Sunflower, Daisy, and Rose when they stop having piglets."

Yeah, I'm sure it's going to be exactly like that. With luck, summer will be over long before Cleo becomes a chicken filet. I wonder if all big-city girls are as clueless about farm life as Laurel is. Where does she think those hot dogs, hamburgers, and pork chops she loves come from? Someday she'll have to hear the hard facts about how animals are turned into food, but it won't be from me.

Just to be sure, I change the subject. "So what's the story with you and Steve, the farmer's son?"

"He turned out to be kind of a dud." Laurel sighs. "Not a bad kisser, though. As if I have anyone to compare him with."

"You? I'm so starved for affection that I get excited when Carmine licks my leg!"

"That's disgusting. Speaking of Carmine, any ideas what we should do about Buttferk?"

Just hearing Laurel say "we" makes me feel better. Too bad it doesn't do a thing to solve our problem.

"I wish I knew."

The next morning, as I'm getting Sammy settled into

his stroller, Miss Simmons seizes my arm in a death grip. "Aspen Parks, tell your obnoxious friends to stop driving past my house! They're getting on my nerves."

For one misguided second, my heart jumps, as I think it might be Clay. My head snaps up but all I see is Ferret's rust bucket pulling away. His windows are down, and the other two members of the Buttferk gang are gawking like tourists.

I channel my thoughts toward summoning a swarm of locusts to attack them. A lone fly buzzes by, but Ferret's car is already gone.

"Believe me, Miss Simmons, none of those losers are my friends. The jury's still out on whether or not they're human." Sammy nuzzles against my palm, and I scratch his head.

I remember what Ferret said about old ladies hoarding valuables. "You keep your doors locked, don't you?"

"Of course. Every minute of the day and night." She nods so vigorously that I'm afraid she'll lose her glasses. "Why? Are you getting ideas about kidnapping my Sammy Stripers?"

"What?"

"I see how you are—trying to lure him away from me with your cooing and petting!"

"Miss Simmons, I-I'd never—"

"Gotcha!" She chuckles, and her face wrinkles like an accordion. "I had you going there for a minute, didn't I?"

Miss Simmons pulled a joke on me! What's next—cows tap-dancing on the moon?

"I have to admit it—you did. But nobody could come between you and Sammy."

She smiles and strokes his head. "You're right, of course. Sammy and I are like two peas in a pod."

Not the way I'd put it, but whatever makes her happy.

"The thing is, Miss Simmons, those aren't nice guys. You said they drive by. Have they ever, uh, said anything to you?"

"They did, and I couldn't believe the audacity!" Her eyes flash. "They wanted to know what was in the baby carriage."

A shiver runs down my back. "What did you tell them?"

"I told them it was none of their damn business!" Miss Simmons smacks her walker on the front porch for emphasis.

"That was . . . good. But if they ask again, maybe you could say it's one of those dolls. You know, the ones that almost look alive?"

Miss Simmons rears her head back. "Like those horrid things I saw on *60 Minutes* last year?"

I swallow. "Well, yes."

"I will not!" She smacks the walker again. "Why, the whole neighborhood would think I'm a crackpot!"

My mouth opens and closes like a fish's, marooned on dry land. I recognize a no-win situation when I see one.

nineteen

A WEEK LATER, I'M SITTING ON THE DECK AFTER DINNER swatting mosquitoes, watching the fireflies, and listening to June bugs hurling themselves at the porch lights. The way I figure it, any June bugs that haven't figured out the workings of a lightbulb by the end of July should give it up and move on. Then again, summer is two-thirds over, and I'm still pining for Clay. So who am I to judge?

Carmine is curled at the top of the steps, snoring. I've been keeping him tied up like Mom suggested, but I'm beginning to think it isn't necessary. Being shot in the butt seems to have cured Carmine of his wandering ways for now. I hate to think he's going to have to be tied up forever.

Since Buttferk have all graduated, why are they still hanging around Cottonwood Creek? It would be one thing if they were going to college in the fall. Since they barely made it out of high school, that doesn't seem likely. So why haven't they gone into the big, bad world, looking for gainful employment? There aren't any jobs in Cottonwood Creek—if anyone was stupid enough to hire them.

The back door opens, and Manny walks out, wearing a ragged Cottonwood Creek High T-shirt and paint-spattered shorts. He sits beside Carmine and lays a hand on his back. "How're you feeling, old guy?" Carmine's tail thumps in response. "Better, huh?"

Manny scratches Carmine just above his tail, and he moans with pleasure. "I'd like to get my hands on the scumbag who shot him."

I've debated telling Manny, but I haven't for just that reason. Sure, he could kick Ferret's butt with his hands duct-taped together. And one-on-one he could probably hold his own with Buster and Kong. But they'd get their revenge one way or another. Then they'd run Carmine down for good measure.

"Yeah, me too." There's nothing else I can say on the subject, so I take a drink from my can of pop. It's luke-warm, and I think something might have been floating in it. Too late now.

Manny idly drums his fingers on the deck. "Clay asked about you the other day."

"He did?" I choke on the insect I seem to have swallowed. "Wh-What did he say?"

Manny shrugs. "He asked if you're ever getting off punishment. For some unknown reason, Clay's still interested in you."

"Really?" I try my best to sound indifferent. "I expected him to be dating someone else by now."

"He's taken Wynter out a couple of times, if that's what you want to know." Manny scratches his head and yawns. "Tessa and I doubled with them once."

"Clay is dating Wynter Green?" I'm going to be sick. "Since when?"

"A few weeks. She and Tessa play golf at the club, so they stop by and talk. You know."

Steam spurts from my ears. "Oh, yeah. I know all right."

"What can I say?" Manny leans back on his hands. "Wynter's hot and she asked Clay out. A guy's got needs."

"Don't give me that crap about a guy's needs!" I aim a kick at him, but he dodges it. "And since when have you been dating Tessa?"

"Tessa and I spend time together, but we're not dating." Manny grins. "She expressed an interest, and I complied. And, despite her lack of accessories"—he cups his hands on his chest—"she has certain talents I appreciate."

My aim is better the second time. "You're disgusting!"

"Ouch!" Manny rubs his side. "Hey, don't kill the messenger! You and Laurel screwed things up, not Clay and me."

"Laurel?"

"She's cute in her own way," he says matter-of-factly. "Kind of out there, but she has a personality. She's not a clone like most of the girls I know."

This is interesting news. "You've thought about her, haven't you?"

"It doesn't matter. Laurel's grounded until whenever, so nothing's going to happen on that front." Manny stands up and heads through the back door. "I'll have to console myself with Tessa and her many and varied talents."

I hurl my empty pop can at him, but it bounces harmlessly against the wall.

Three more weeks of my crappy life crawl by, and somehow it's the eighteenth of August. The magnificent summer before my senior year is nearly over, and nothing good has come of it. I haven't seen or heard from Clay, which means, I guess, that he's gotten over being "interested" in me. No doubt he and Wynter will be announcing their engagement at his family's Labor Day picnic.

The fur on Carmine's bald spot is growing back in. I've stopped tying him up in the backyard, and, as far as I can tell, he's been staying there. Lately there haven't been any Buttferk sightings while I'm walking Sammy. So, I guess two good things have happened.

Laurel and I still talk every day, which is easier now that our parents have let up a little on our restrictions. She wasn't as excited as I thought she'd be when I told her about Manny's possible interest in her. Mostly she rattled on about Cleo, her almost-pet chicken. It's pretty sad when that's the most exciting thing someone as perky as Laurel has to talk about.

I'm giving myself a week of vacation before school begins on August twenty-sixth. Laurel told me school in Chicago doesn't start until the middle of September, but in Iowa it always begins right after the State Fair. Since today was my last day at the Sub Stop, I had to endure a rambling speech from Willie about what a dependable employee I've been—except for my brief lapse in judgment earlier this summer—and how proud he was to have played a part in putting me back on the straight and narrow.

Whew! I had no idea how close I'd come to living a life of dissipation and crime. I should probably send Willie a bouquet of french fries as a thank-you gift. The next time I hit the drive-through at Burger King, I'll pick some up.

twenty

SOMETHING YANKS ME AWAKE. I LOOK AT MY CLOCK AND RELAX
back against my pillow. It's just after midnight, which
means I have twelve more hours to sleep. I told Miss
Simmons that I won't be taking Sammy for his walk
until tomorrow—I mean this—afternoon. Her hip is so
much better that she's hoping to walk part of the way
with us. But that's at least twelve long, peaceful hours
from now.

Hail peppers against my window like tiny rocks. That's
probably what woke me up. Moonlight sends shadows
across my bedspread, almost as bright as day. How can it
be hailing on a clear night?

Another shower of little somethings clinks against the

glass. Could Clay be tossing pebbles at my window to lure me into his waiting arms?

I smooth my hair and hurry to look out. Someone is standing on our lawn, bathed romantically in moonlight. But this someone is much shorter than Clay. And has way bigger boobs.

As quietly as possible, I crank open the window. "Laurel!" I whisper-shout. "What are you doing?"

"Come down here!" Her voice is hoarse with tears. "It's a matter of life and death!"

Not this time. I will not be lured to my doom by another of Laurel's life-and-death emergencies. I begin to crank in reverse.

"Please, Aspen! They're going to murder Cleo!" Whatever else Laurel tries to say is lost in her wild sobbing.

Too bad I don't get paid for predicting the future of Laurel's animal friends. I could use the extra money to bail myself out of jail. But this summer's in the toilet, anyway, and Mom and Dad can't ground me from school.

"Hold on, Laurel. I'm coming down." Remembering the pig fiasco, I take a second to pull on an extra T-shirt over my sleep tee. And I put on my sneakers instead of flip-flops. Who says I don't learn from my mistakes?

Carmine has been watching me with interest, but this is one adventure I'm having without him. "Sorry, buddy, I have to lock you in." I back toward the bedroom door, prepared to fight my way out of the room. But he just expels a huge sigh and lays his head on his paws.

At least one of us has developed some common sense.

It's almost scary how good I've become at sneaking out of the house. In less than a minute I'm in the backyard. I find Laurel leaning against the house with her arms crossed over her chest, her cheeks gleaming with tears. When she sees me, she flings herself against me, sobbing.

This isn't Laurel being a drama queen. I pat her back and let her cry until she winds down. With all the noise she's making, I expect Mom and Dad to switch on the outdoor lights and catch us.

"Okay," I say when she finally stops crying. "Tell me what's going on. And why didn't you call instead of throwing rocks at my window?"

"I forgot to put my phone on the charger." Laurel rubs her face with her T-shirt sleeve. "I'll tell you the rest on the way there. My car's parked in the alley."

I open the gate and seal my doom. "On the way where?" The question is just a formality because I already know what she's going to say.

"EggstraGood, of course. Those murderers!" She blows her nose on a crumpled tissue.

It's a typical August night, muggy, still, and smelling of freshly cut grass. A hummingbird moth dips its nose into the lily-shaped flowers of Mom's sprawling moonflower plant. The only sounds I hear are Laurel honking her nose and air-conditioners humming. Our shadows are surprisingly clear, thanks to the full moon.

This is the first time I've seen Laurel's car, which is small, white, and nondescript. As I climb in, I notice the empty cat carrier on the backseat and remember a line from an old western, something about shooting chicken thieves.

"Okay, we're on our way. Tell me what's going on."

Laurel waits to answer until we pull away from the curb. "Today at work, a couple of the workers starting separating the green chickens from all the other ones."

"Green chickens? I know chickens come in different colors, but green?"

Laurel shakes her head at my lack of knowledge about all things poultry. "The chickens aren't green, Aspen. They have green tags on their wings." She turns onto a gravel road. "When I started working at EggstraGood, Steve explained that the tags show when the chickens were hatched so the people at the farm know which ones are the oldest."

"Let me guess. Cleo is in the oldest group of chickens."

Laurel bites her lower lip and nods. Her eyes well up with tears. "And tomorrow they're going to pack them into trucks and send them off to be slaughtered."

"Wait a minute. One chicken can't cost very much. Why didn't you just offer to buy . . . Cleo?"

"I did." Laurel sniffles. "But Steve and his father are off fishing at some stupid lake in northern Canada and can't be reached. And when I asked the jerk manager who's in charge until they get back, he said he's not authorized to 'sell the stock to anyone except pre-approved buyers.'" Tears roll down her cheeks.

"Just so I understand, we're only rescuing Cleo, right? Because if you're talking about letting the whole flock go, I'm out."

Laurel stares at the road so long I start to ask her again. "Yes, just Cleo." She dabs her eyes. "I just wish I hadn't gotten to know all the girls personally. It's so hard. . . ."

I remember the five fuzzy yellow chicks my science class hatched in third grade. They lived in a cage in the classroom until they got too big and messy for our teacher, Ms. Voss, to take care of. She gave them to her farmer fiancé to supposedly live out their lives in peace and harmony. It made perfect sense to a bunch of nine-year-olds, but those chickens probably ended up as their Sunday dinner.

"Yeah, it is," I agree, thinking of those cute little chicks, "but that's what happens to farm animals when they've outlived their usefulness. I know it seems cruel, but farmers can't afford to keep feeding animals that don't produce."

Laurel's grip on the wheel gets tighter. "So Daisy, Sunflower, and Rose are going to be killed, too?"

Baby steps. We're taking baby steps. "Nah. Those three will spend their days hanging out in the pig pen, slapping mud packs on their faces, and debating which hog has the hunkiest physique."

A hint of a smile crosses Laurel's face. We ride in silence for a few minutes until the EggstraGood Farm sign appears on our left. Laurel turns off the gravel road onto the asphalt driveway. Then she cuts the lights and engine and we coast until we're out of sight of the main road.

"Okay, as far as I know, there isn't a night security guy," Laurel says. "All we have to do is climb over the fence, grab Cleo, and get out of there."

"As far as you know?"

Laurel lifts the cat carrier over the seat back and onto her lap. "Well, I couldn't exactly come out and ask, now could I?"

"I guess not." There's no point in arguing with Laurel when she's like this. "So, how high is this fence? Is it barbed wire?"

"It's not that high, and it's not barbed wire." She opens her door. "As soon as we walk over there, you can see for yourself."

And I was worried that Laurel hadn't thought this through.

We walk together up the winding asphalt driveway. Fluffy clouds roll across the moon, bathing us in alternating light and shadow. The pungent odor of chicken poop coats the inside of my nose, and a rank river of sweat pours between my shoulder blades. None of the smells bother me that much because I'm too scared to breathe.

When they snap my picture for the Wanted poster, I hope they get my good side.

To our left is a gigantic red barn with a white EggstraGood sign on the side. Laurel veers off the driveway and across a mowed pasture. We stumble over chopped-off weed stalks and hidden rabbit holes until we reach the fence surrounding the chicken yard.

Laurel is right about the fence. It's only about five feet tall and it's not barbed wire. But the red and black warning sign is pretty significant. "Didn't you know it's an electric fence?"

"That sign's just to scare people. I've leaned against this fence a hundred times and never been shocked." Laurel sets the cat carrier on the ground and grabs the top wire. "See? Nothing happens." She throws her leg over the top. "After I climb over, hand me—"

Laurel shoots backward and lands on her butt in the weeds. "Crap! Crap! Crap!" she moans as she rubs her inner thigh.

"Are you okay?"

"What do you think?" she snaps, checking her leg for damage. "I was almost electrocuted."

I help her up. "Electric fences won't kill you. They just give a strong enough jolt to keep out predators. I imagine this one is only on at night."

Laurel jerks her hand away. "Thank you, Bill Nye, the Science Guy. If you know so much, what do we do now?"

"Since you're getting testy with me, you can take me home and figure it out for yourself." I turn on my heel and head back across the field.

"Wait, Aspen! Please!" Laurel rushes after me. "I'm sorry. I didn't mean it. I'm just so worried about Cleo."

"Well, don't take it out on me." I stumble on a weed stalk and mentally curse myself for getting sucked into another of her schemes. "This is your chicken rescue, not mine."

"I know, and I said I was sorry. Now will you please come back with me?"

I keep walking. "Not yet. We can't get over the fence unless we can get past the electric current."

"That makes sense." Laurel is clearly trying to get on my good side. "So I drive the car up to the fence, we climb on the hood, and jump over. But how do we get back?"

"Bill Nye would be very disappointed in you." I open the passenger door and check out the floor mats, which, as I'd hoped, are rubber. "I don't suppose there's any duct tape in here?"

"Dad put together an emergency kit, but I've never opened it." Laurel flips the trunk release under her dashboard. "It's in the trunk."

When we open the Rubbermaid box in the back of Laurel's car, I say a prayer of thanks for the male obsession with duct tape. Laurel and I pull the four floor mats out of her car and haul them back to the fence along with the two rolls of duct tape from her emergency kit. We rip the tape with our teeth—probably undoing my two years of wearing braces—and fasten all four mats together.

Thanks to Laurel, we know that the top wire isn't electric. So we drape the mats over the second wire from the top so that they hang down and cover both sides of the fence. The mats don't quite reach the ground, so we're going to have to be extra careful not to touch the bottom wire, just in case.

"Okay, guinea pig," I tell Laurel. "You first."

She rubs her palms on her shorts, takes a deep breath, and grabs the top wire. I give her a boost until she's straddling the fence. Then she maneuvers her right leg over and drops down on the other side.

"That was brilliant, Aspen!" She pumps her fist in the air. "I promise never to make fun of you or Bill Nye again."

"As your future cellmate, I'm going to hold you to that." I hand her the cat carrier. Getting over the fence with no help from behind is tricky. I have to shinny over on my stomach, turn around, and slide down the mats on the other side.

When I'm safely over the fence, I eyeball Laurel to make sure she's not secretly recording me. If this shows up on YouTube, she's a dead woman.

twenty-one

WITH THE FENCE BEHIND US, LAUREL AND I WALK ACROSS THE chicken park to the barns where they roost. According to her, the green chickens are in the building that's farthest from the fence. Of course they are.

Aside from the sound of chicken poop squishing under our feet, everything is quiet. No security guards rush out waving guns. No Rottweilers or pit bulls attack us with dripping jaws. No floodlights snap on to illuminate our wrongdoing.

Our little misdemeanor is going too smoothly, and it's making my skin crawl. We've forgotten something critical, but what?

"Okay, Laurel. Walk me through this." Even though

nobody's around, I can't help but whisper. "Once we're inside the chicken house, what's going to happen?"

She brushes an insect away from her face. "I pick up Cleo and put her in the carrier. Then we leave."

Now I know what we've forgotten. "How are you going to tell her apart from all the other chickens?"

Laurel smiles. "That's easy. You can't see them in the dark, but there are red plastic streamers tied around some of these fence posts. Before I left today, I sneaked one of them off and tied it around the tag on Cleo's wing."

"But if we can't see the streamers out here in the dark, how will we see the one on her wing?"

She stops with her hand on the chicken house door-knob and glares at me. "Why are you always so critical of my ideas?"

Because they suck?

The door swings open and I follow Laurel inside. It's at least ten degrees warmer in here. Dust hangs in the air, and the chicken-poop smell is overpowering. Except for moonlight slipping through crank-out windows near the ceiling, the huge building is dark. Even so, I can see feathery lumps sitting wing to wing on shoulder-high roosts from one end of the building to the other.

"Okay, Laurel." Sarcasm is leaking from my pores. "Grab your good friend Cleo and we're out of here."

Laurel turns slowly, taking in the hundreds of snoozing

hens. "I didn't know there'd be so many," she wails, "and it's so dark. I'll never find Cleo now."

The chickens nearest to us rustle their feathers and make sleepy clucking sounds. Their restlessness is contagious, traveling along the roost like an old-fashioned game of telephone.

"Shh! You're waking them up."

Laurel covers her mouth with her hands, but that doesn't stop tears from dripping down her cheeks. Even though I'm pissed, I can't help feeling sorry for her. Besides, I didn't risk my freedom to come away empty-handed.

"Pull yourself together, Laurel," I hiss in her ear. "Cleo's life depends on it."

She takes a deep breath and wipes her face with the heels of her hands.

"Good. Now, imagine that Cleo is hanging out with the other . . . girls, and you're trying to get her attention. What do you do?"

"Nothing. I mean, when she sees me in the yard, she just runs over to me."

Be patient. Violence is not the answer.

"Okay, but suppose she's looking the other way. Then what?"

Laurel shakes her head sadly. "Seriously, I don't do anything." Then her face lights up. "Wait. She likes it when I whistle."

Now we're getting somewhere. "So Cleo comes when you whistle?"

"No. Not really," Laurel says. "But sometimes she sings along."

Why am I not surprised? "Whatever works. Pucker up and go to it."

So help me, if Laurel asks what tune she should whistle, I'll wring her neck. But, either she senses my mood or she and Cleo have a favorite song. She licks her lips and starts whistling.

The chickens closest to us are unimpressed, so Laurel begins walking along the roosts. I walk behind her, watching the chickens for signs of musical talent. Because of all the dust, Laurel has to keep stopping in mid-whistle to muster up more spit. At this rate, she's going to run out of saliva before Cleo chimes in with her part of the duet. Unless this human/chicken bonding is another figment of Laurel's wild imagination.

Walking through a barn full of snoozing chickens is a major snore. My eyes are drooping and I can't stop yawning. Every time I do, about a hundred gnats fly into my mouth. It's during that quiet time between yawning and spitting out gnats that I hear a faint *"bawk, bawk."*

I grab Laurel's arm and hold my finger to my lips. Then I circle my index finger near my mouth and nod for her to begin whistling. One silent step at a time we move forward, and I hear the *bawking* again. While Laurel keeps whistling, I track the *bawk* to the far end of the roost. Looking closely, I see a scrap of ribbon hanging from one of the hens' wings.

Cleo would never make it past the first round of *American Idol* auditions, but her *bawk* is music to my ears.

Laurel slides her hands under Cleo's stomach and lifts her from the roost. I hold my breath, expecting chicken hell to break loose, but Cleo doesn't raise a squawk. She seems content to snuggle into Laurel's arms and go back to sleep.

I let out a long breath of relief that we've made it this far. "Okay, you've got her. Let's go."

With Cleo cuddled against her, Laurel looks up and down the long rows of sleeping chickens. "Good-bye, girls," she whispers. "I'm sorry I can't save all of you. But I promise I'll never eat chicken again for the rest of my life."

As much as I love Mom's fried chicken, I silently take the pledge, too. I couldn't chomp down on a creature I've practically had a sleepover with. Then I pick up the cat carrier by the handle, hold Laurel's upper arm, and steer her toward the door. "Don't look back. That will only make it worse."

Outdoors, all is still quiet although thick clouds have obscured the moon. Laurel snuffles and wipes her eyes on Cleo's back.

"Don't you want to put Cleo in the carrier?"

"No. Let's wait until we get to the fence." Laurel scratches Cleo under the chin . . . beak . . . whatever. "I don't thi—"

A monstrous, dark shape whooshes past our heads, startling her to silence. It passes so close that the breeze from its wings stirs my hair.

I start to say, "What was that?" when Cleo sets up a frantic chatter, squirms out of Laurel's arms, and hits the ground running. Wings flapping, she zigzags across the chicken park, squawking her beak off.

"No, Cleo! Wait!" Laurel shouts, taking off after her. But it's clear from the start that her running is no match for Cleo's wing-assisted velocity. I drop the carrier and go wide, trying to cut Cleo off before she ducks through the fence and escapes. It doesn't look promising.

The owl swoops in on enormous wings, its round yellow eyes gleaming. It plunges toward the screeching Cleo, who is circling back toward us.

Laurel screams and shields her face. I cover my eyes.

There's a rush of wind, followed by a blood-curdling squawk and a thud. Then silence.

I uncover my eyes, steeling myself for the sight of Cleo's twisted and blood-soaked body. But except for a few stray feathers, there's nothing. The owl made a clean kill and carried her away. At least Laurel is spared the sight of her friend's bloody corpse.

Laurel's face is buried in her hands, and her shoulders are heaving. My arms hang helplessly at my sides. After all we went through, we still lost Cleo.

"Laurel, I'm so sorry." It sounds lame even to me, but

there's nothing else to say. I walk over and pull her head against my shoulder. The raw sobs tearing from her throat bring tears to my eyes, too.

To everyone except Laurel, Cleo was just a chicken. But we love who we love—an annoying friend, a goofy dog, a spoiled-rotten skunk, even a plain old chicken. And losing who we love hurts like hell.

"Come on. Let's get out of here." Laurel's crying so hard, I don't think she can hear me. I pat her shoulder and ease her away from me. Every second we stay puts us in danger of being caught. I'll feel much better when we're over the fence and off EggstraGood property. If Laurel's too upset, I can drive us home.

Wearily, I shuffle over to pick up the cat carrier. The wire door popped open when I dropped it. I crouch to close it and see a shape inside.

"Cleo?" I murmur, and hear a muffled *bawk*. I'm not fluent in poultry, but it sounds like a *bawk* of relief to me.

"Cleo's in the cat carrier! I think she's okay!"

Laurel's there in an instant. She pulls Cleo out and pats her from head to tail. "Oh, thank you! Thank you!" she says over and over as she hugs the chicken.

I say a silent prayer of thanks. "Now we're seriously getting out of here. But this time Cleo goes in the carrier—and stays there."

twenty-two

I DON'T BEGIN TO RELAX UNTIL WE'RE OUT OF THE EggstraGood driveway and heading toward town. "So, now that we've rescued Cleo, what are you going to do with her?"

Laurel glances into the backseat, where Cleo seems to be resting comfortably inside the carrier. "I'm going to keep her, of course. If I take good care of her, she can live to be fourteen years old. I read that on the Internet."

"That's great, but she can't live in your house. And how are you going to explain her to your dad? I guarantee he won't fall for the old 'She followed me home. Can I keep her?' line."

"All right, maybe I haven't quite thought it all the

way through," Laurel says. "But I didn't have a lot of time to plan it out." As we reach the Cottonwood Creek city limits, she eases off the gas. "For tonight she can stay in the shed where we keep the lawn mower."

At least Cleo is Laurel's problem now and not mine. I'm still in shock that we actually pulled something off without Officer Sierra catching us and hauling us away to jail. Or Buttferk—

My stomach lurches. "Slow down, Laurel. Isn't that Buster's truck?"

We slow to a crawl alongside the pickup parked on the street. Its scabby paint job looks sickeningly familiar. "What's his truck doing here?" Laurel asks. "The rock he lives under is on the other side of town."

I flash back to Ferret in the Sub Stop drive-through making threats against my dog and my family. "But my house is just two blocks from here." What if my bedroom door didn't latch? Carmine could have nosed his way out and gone looking for me.

"Do you think he's after Carmine?" Sometimes Laurel has an uncanny way of reading my mind. She steps on the gas, and a minute later we're pulling into the alley behind my house. I jump out of the car almost before it stops moving.

"I'm coming, too, in case you need help." Laurel closes the car door behind her and double-checks to make sure it's locked. As we're hurrying to the back gate, I look up at my bedroom window. That was brilliant—I forgot to turn off my lamp.

Someone is leaning on my windowsill, looking out over our backyard. My chest twists with rage. Buster is in my bedroom, going through my stuff, probably trying on my underwear! I'll kill that—

The intruder turns, giving me a clear look at his profile: his long nose, floppy ears, and the little ruff of fur around his neck. I let out a long breath. "They're not here. If something was wrong, Carmine would be going nuts."

"So everything's okay. Good deal." Laurel rubs her eyes. "I can't wait to go home and fall into bed. I'm dead on my feet."

"Our house seems to be okay." I remember Ferret's greasy smile while he listed the treasures he's sure Miss Simmons is hoarding. "But they may be after Miss Simmons. We've got to check on her."

"Crap!" Laurel turns on her heels. "You're right!"

We run to the end of the alley, jog to the corner, and start across the street. A black car races from out of nowhere and screeches to a stop in the intersection, cutting us off.

Manny gets out of his car and stands in front of us, looking like a traffic cop with his legs spread and his hands on his hips. "Holy crap, Aspen! Haven't you two been arrested enough this summer?"

"Stuff it, Manny." I'm too tired and stressed to deal with him now. I sidestep him and ignore Clay, who's gotten out of the passenger seat. Nothing tops off a special evening like running into my crush on his way home from a date at two thirty in the morning.

Laurel blocks me with her arm. "Aspen, tell them what's going on. If Miss Simmons is in trouble, they can help."

My gaze travels past Manny's self-righteous smirk to Clay, who's watching me with an expression I can't quite read. Concern? Embarrassment because he's been on another date with Wynter?

I can't worry about that now. "Get your car out of the street, and I'll tell you while we walk."

But when I try to explain my concern about Miss Simmons, Manny shoots me down. "You've been sniffing too much burger grease, Sis. That old beater of Buster's probably broke down, and he doesn't have the bucks to have it towed. There's your big conspiracy."

"Don't be too quick to blow it off, Manny. I've seen those jerks stalking Miss Simmons, too." Clay hitches his chinos up on his cute butt. "It won't hurt to check it out."

Manny grumbles, but it's three against one. Not to

mention that we're already standing on Miss Simmons's front walk. No house lights are visible from here, and the only sound is the mosquitoes whining in my ears. One of them lands on my arm, and I smush it.

"See? Nothing's happening." Manny waves mosquitoes away from his face. "Now can we go?"

"Let's make sure the back door looks okay first." Clay surprises me by taking my arm. "You should stay close—in case there's trouble."

I can't argue with that logic.

The four of us slip past the honeysuckle hedge along Miss Simmons's driveway. Until now, I hadn't noticed how overgrown it is. I'll bring our trimmers over tomorrow and give it a few whacks. Miss Simmons may be ready to graduate to a three-pronged cane, but she's not in any shape for yard work.

When we reach her backyard, I hear a muffled thud, but I can't tell where it's coming from. Shiny, odd-shaped pieces of something glitter on the concrete steps leading to her kitchen door. Clay's hand on my arm tenses. My attention moves up the steps, and I see what he sees— Miss Simmons's kitchen door is ajar.

Miss Simmons never leaves her door unlocked.

A weak beam of light glowing from inside the house highlights a still form sprawled on the kitchen floor. Next to the form, a walker lies on its side, just out of reach.

"Call 9-1-1!" I yell as I bound up the stairs. Poor Miss Simmons has had a heart attack or stroke. I hope she's not—

Oof!

Something heavy hits me on the shoulder, dropping me to my knees on the floor next to her. On the way down I see a pair of legs the size of telephone poles. A hand winds in my hair and jerks my head back, and I'm looking into Kong's gigantic, hairy nostrils. Tears of pain fill my eyes.

"Get your hands off her!" Clay yells as he dives over me and into Kong's stomach. Kong stumbles back, releasing my hair—most of it anyway. He and Clay fall to the floor in a grunting tumble of arms and legs.

I crawl to Miss Simmons and put three fingers on her neck the way they do on TV. At first I can't feel anything, but just above her collarbone I find her pulse. I don't know enough to say if it's strong or weak, but her heart is beating.

As I'm about to yell for help to Manny, he sprints past me. Ferret and Buster have appeared from somewhere in the house, and they're trying to kick Clay while Kong holds him down. Manny topples Buster in mid-kick, and Ferret scurries out of the way.

"I called 9-1-1 and asked for the paramedics and the police," Laurel says between panting breaths. "Is she . . . ?"

"She's alive." I see a huge bump on Miss Simmons's forehead. Her eyelids are quivering, but I don't know whether she's conscious. "We've got to get her out of here before she gets trampled."

The guys are shoving and throwing punches. Their bodies slam into each other, the walls, and the furniture. Buster bangs against a cabinet, rattling the dishes in the drainer by the sink. A cup rolls off the countertop and smashes to pieces on the floor. There's no time to lose.

Moving Miss Simmons probably isn't the best idea, but if Kong stomps on her head, she'll be in much worse shape than she is now. "I'll grab her under the arms; you lift her legs." I lay Miss Simmons's arms across her chest, then squat above her head and slide my arms under her shoulders. Laurel does the same with her knees.

"Okay, one, two, three." We lift Miss Simmons and carry her outside. Her left arm slips off and drags on the floor. For such a small person, she's really heavy. By the time we get her down the steps and onto the lawn, my arms are trembling.

Now that Miss Simmons is safe, I'm worried about Clay and Manny. In most cases, I'd call it three against two, but Kong counts for a person and a half—probably more since they're all dirty fighters.

Laurel gives me a shake. "OMG, that looks like smoke!" She points toward a half-open window on the far end of the house. A thin trail of smoke wriggles through the screen like a witch's bony finger.

Miss Simmons's eyes flutter open and she gropes for my hand. "Sammy," she murmurs, "save my Sammy."

"Is he in his cage?" But her eyes have already closed. "Call the fire department, too!" I tell Laurel as I race back into the house.

Why don't I hear any sirens yet? All summer long we've been tripping over Officer Sierra. Now, when we need him, he's not around.

As soon as I'm in the kitchen, I smell the smoke, which seems to be coming from a room down the hall. Manny is straddling Kong's chest, and Clay is sitting on his legs. Kong is breathing hard, but for the moment he's not putting up a fight. Buster is slumped against the kitchen wall, apparently out cold. Ferret seems to have ducked out during the fighting. No surprise there.

"Are the cops on their way?" Manny asks through swollen lips. "We could use some help here."

"They should be here any minute. Laurel called them." I step around the pile of male bodies and stop at the end of the hall. "You guys need to get out of here ASAP. I think there's a fire on the other side of the house."

"A fire?" Clay raises his head and sniffs. "Go back out where it's safe, Aspen. We'll be there in a second."

He looks at Manny over Kong's bulging stomach.

"We've got to haul these guys out of here. We should . . ."

While the guys are discussing how to get Kong and Buster outdoors without letting them escape, I slip into the hallway. It's dark and narrow, with old pictures hanging on the walls. The thickening smoke makes it that much harder to see where I'm going.

The first room on my left is a bathroom. No place for Sammy to hide here. I grab a hand towel hanging by the sink and soak it with water. Another safety tip I've seen on TV.

The next room holds an ironing board and a sewing machine as well as the usual bedroom furniture. It's a mess, with drawers pulled out and overturned onto the floor. I'm holding the wet towel over my nose and mouth, but my eyes are watering like crazy. Sirens are wailing outside, and red, blue, and yellow lights strobe through the windows. The chaos has to be freaking Sammy out. I drop the towel and get down on my hands and knees.

Calling for Sammy, I crawl through the wreckage of sewing supplies, spare bedding, and miscellaneous old-person stuff. Then I peer under the bed and check the closet. No Sammy here, either. I stagger to my feet and move on.

As far as I can tell, there's only one more room off this hallway, and that has to be Miss Simmons's bed-room. Smoke billows from the doorway, clouding my vision and clogging my lungs. I lower my head and hurry forward. If I don't find Sammy soon, I'll have to give up.

The drapes beside her bed are smoldering, but the flames seem to be having a hard time of it, so maybe they're made of some flame-retardant fabric. The flowered wallpaper is curling from the heat, and sparks are flying onto her bedspread. It's going to start burning any second.

Smoke sears my lungs, and my throat feels like it's on fire. I drop to all fours again. "Good, Sammy. Here, Sammy." My voice cracks from the heat and smoke.

I lift the dust ruffle and peer under Miss Simmons's bed. Two yellow points of light look back at me, and I almost collapse with relief.

I stretch my arm under the bed and wriggle my fingers. "Hey, Sammy. It's okay, boy. Come to Aspen." He inches forward. "Good boy, Sammy. Come on."

Something huge crashes to the floor. I jerk my head out from under the bed, hitting it on the bed frame. On the floor nearby are the curtain rod and the charred remains of drapes. From underneath the bed, Sammy is chattering. Not a good sign.

I duck back under the dust ruffle. Sammy's tail is straight in the air and he's doing a stiff-legged dance. "Shush. It's okay, Sammy. Come here, baby."

I slither under the bed, stringing together wordless cooing sounds until Sammy's tail relaxes. When I think

I'm no longer in danger of being bitten or squirted, I reach out and scratch him under the chin. Then I work my other hand around his middle and slide him with me as I scoot backward.

When I'm finally out, I cup his body against my chest and use the bedspread to pull myself up. The holes where the sparks have landed are glowing and expanding. Flames from the burning drapes are licking at the dust ruffle on the side of the bed nearest the window.

"We are so out of here, Sammy." I'd like to find his carrier, but the smoke and heat are too much for me. I spin around and—

Ferret is forming a subhuman door. His feet are spread at maximum width, and he's latched on to both sides of the doorframe. "Hah! I knew you'd come back for the good stuff!"

Give me a freaking break.

Turning to the side to protect Sammy, I lower my shoulder and plow into Ferret's chest. He folds at the waist and collapses backward onto his butt. Since I can still see his beady eyes, he's conscious, which means he can get out of here under his own power.

Spitting smoke, I hurdle over him. The scummy little vermin seizes my ankle and I go sprawling, letting go of Sammy to break my fall. He lands on all fours, but my elbow hits the bare wood floor.

Agony shoots up my arm and blows out the top of

my head. Rage roars in behind the pain. I leap to my feet with every intention of stomping Ferret into rodent paste.

But Sammy is already doing his stiff-legged dance, and his business end is aimed at Ferret. Ferret tries to scramble to his feet, but it's too late. Sammy squirts a stream of liquid from his behind into Ferret's eyes.

Ferret lets out a squeal that would make Sunflower blush. Skunk stench mixes with the dense smoke to form a suffocating toxic soup. I scoop Sammy into my arms and dash down the hall toward the kitchen.

Two firefighters in full gear step out of Miss Simmons's sewing room, and I nearly drop Sammy again. "Is anyone else in the house?" one of them asks, his voice muffled by an oxygen mask.

With my free hand, I point toward Miss Simmons's room. "One," I manage to croak.

The firefighter who spoke heads down the hall, while the other one steers me through the kitchen and down the steps to the backyard. Clay shakes off the hand of a large man who's holding his arm and rushes to me. He reaches out to hug me but pulls back when he sees Sammy.

"My God, Aspen! Are you all right?" His left eye is swollen shut, his cheek is purple, and there's a smear of dried blood under his nose. "They wouldn't let me go back in." He takes my upper arm and draws me toward an ambulance parked on Miss Simmons's back lawn.

"I'm fine." I sound like a frog with laryngitis, and my

elbow is throbbing. "But I've got to get Sammy out of here before someone sees him."

Clay makes a sharp right turn to the alley. "We'll put him in the cab of my truck for now. Then you're going to let the paramedics take a look at you."

"What about you? Your face is a mess."

"If you think we look bad, you should see Buster and Kong." Manny startles me by falling into step with us. Laurel, looking much fresher than I feel, is snuggled under his arm. Manny's nose is bandaged, both eyes are black, and his lips look like summer sausages. "I'm glad you're okay. I came this close to getting worried about you." He holds his thumb and index finger an inch apart.

Laurel elbows Manny in the side. "You should have seen these guys freak out when the firemen wouldn't let them go in after you." If I had the energy, I'd wonder why those two are suddenly so chummy.

"Thanks, guys." I cough, and I swear a puff of smoke comes out my mouth. "Uh, Laurel. Clay and I are taking Miss Simmons's cat to his truck for safekeeping. That might be a good place to put your new . . . pet, too."

Manny cranes his neck to look at Sammy. "That doesn't look like any cat I've ever seen." His eyes grow as wide as possible, considering all the swelling. "What the . . . ! It's a sku—"

"If anyone asks, he's Miss Simmons's pet cat, Sammy Stripers," Laurel interrupts him. "And Clay is keeping him at his farm until she's out of the hospital."

The farther we walk from the scene of the fire, the quieter it becomes. I take a deep breath of fresh air and manage to exhale without coughing. I could swear I stumbled around in Miss Simmons's smoke-filled house for hours, but Clay says it's not quite four a.m. Crickets chirp and fireflies glide across the alley, but the mosquitoes are blissfully absent. Maybe it's because we all smell like smoke.

The throbbing in my elbow has settled into a dull ache. Sammy is squirming, so I shift him to my other side. He's getting heavy, and his claws are digging into my arms. "Did you hear how she is?"

"The last I saw of Miss Simmons, she was wide awake and mad as hell." Clay squeezes my arm just enough to let me know he's still holding on. "She wouldn't let the ambulance leave until she told Officer Sierra about the 'three thugs' breaking into her house and knocking her down." He grins. "She's a feisty old gal."

Of course Officer Sierra is in the neighborhood. It wouldn't be a summer night without him. "Did he arrest Buster and Kong?"

"Oh, yeah," Manny says. "Thanks to yours truly and my man here." He reaches across me to bump fists with

Clay. "But that loser Ferret took off when the fighting started. He's probably on his way to Canada."

"Not so much." I tell them how Ferret tried to block my way out—and how Sammy took care of him.

"That's perfect!" Manny whoops with laughter, then he winces. "My face hurts like an SOB."

I stifle my sisterly urge to make a comeback.

twenty-three

BEFORE WE TAKE SAMMY TO CLAY'S TRUCK, WE MAKE A DETOUR to get Cleo out of Laurel's car, which is still parked in the alley behind my house. There's a bright red ticket under her windshield wiper citing her for blocking the right-of-way. She looks disgusted. "I've already gotten about a dozen of these. Who knew the cops in this town would be so picky about where you park?"

Laurel lifts out Cleo's carrier and locks the door again.

"Aren't you going to move your car?" Manny asks.

"Why bother?" Laurel shrugs. "I've already paid for this parking spot." Manny chuckles and tucks her back under his arm. It's a good thing he's going to college for orientation next week. If they became a couple, Cottonwood Creek would be in deep trouble.

As we walk toward Clay's truck, Manny takes the carrier from Laurel. "So what's in here—a possum?"

Laurel cuts a look at me. "No. It's just a little chicken," she says meekly.

"Seriously?" Manny lifts the carrier to eye level and peers in at Cleo. "So it is." His swollen nose and lips make his *s*'s sound like *th*.

My breathing stops while I wait for one of the guys to make the connection.

It hits Clay first. He pulls me up short. "Aren't you working out at the chicken farm?" I can't bring myself to look at him.

"I was . . . sort of." Laurel avoids his gaze. "Yesterday was my last day."

"Let me guess. They gave you one of their chickens as a going-away present?" Clay cocks an eyebrow at her.

"I had to save Cleo. They were going to kill her!" Laurel's eyes well up, but I'm not so sure tears are going to work on Clay.

Clay drops my arm. "And stealing it was all you could come up with?" His good eye is blazing and the muscles in his neck are rigid. "A laying hen is worth—at the most—five bucks. Why didn't you just offer to buy it from them?"

Laurel squares up for an argument. "I tried, but the owner is out of town and the manager wouldn't let me. If I waited until the owner got back, Cleo would be dead."

Clay blows out a frustrated breath. "Okay. I can kind of see your point. But it's not too late to pay for the bird."

Laurel shakes her head. "If I confess and offer to pay for Cleo now, I'll get arrested again."

"Why can't Laurel pay for Cleo without confessing?" Since I'm not brave enough to meet Clay's eyes, I look at his chin. "If she sends EggstraGood five or even ten dollars—anonymously, of course—they get more money than Cleo's worth, Cleo gets to live, and Laurel doesn't get arrested. It's a win-win-win."

"You need to add another 'win' to that list, because her accomplice wouldn't be arrested, either." Clay flashes me a grin and links his arm through mine again.

"Okay, make it four wins." I let out a sigh of relief.

"How about this," he tells Laurel, "you send Eggstra-Good twenty dollars—"

Laurel squeaks but wisely keeps her mouth shut.

"—for . . . Cleo, and we all forget this conversation ever happened."

"It's a deal," I jump in before Laurel says something stupid.

When we get to Clay's pickup, which happens to be parked in front of our house, he takes Cleo's carrier from

Manny and lifts it into the back of his truck. But where to put Sammy is a problem.

"Cleo doesn't take up much room," Laurel says. "We could put Sammy with her in the carrier for now."

Clay snorts. "You really are a city girl. Skunks are predators; chickens are prey. It wouldn't be good for Cleo's health."

We end up making a nest of rags in the passenger seat for Sammy and pulling the bed cover over Cleo's carrier in the back of Clay's truck. We've barely gotten the animals settled when the outdoor lights flip on and my parents barrel out our front door.

What's left of the night is gobbled up by interviews, interrogations, and paramedics. Officer Sierra and the fire department are in charge of the interviews. My parents and Laurel's dad handle the interrogations. The paramedics check us over, put a patch over Clay's eye, and hand out ice packs. My elbow is bruised, but I pass on having it X-rayed. Now that my funny bone isn't sending electric shocks through my nervous system, it doesn't feel that bad. For the first time, Laurel and I won't have a problem telling Officer Sierra the truth about what happened, mainly because he's not interested in where we were before we arrived at Miss Simmons's house.

Too bad our parents don't share his lack of interest. Laurel and I are under eighteen, which means Mom, Dad, and Mr. Piedmont are going to be listening and probably taking notes when we give our statements to Officer Sierra. Mom and Dad astonish us both when they let Laurel drive me to the police station. I guess they figure it's better than leaving her car parked in the alley. Laurel and I take advantage of the time to concoct what we hope is a plausible story about what happened before we went to Miss Simmons's house.

"Since I got you into this, I'll take the blame." Laurel checks the rearview mirror to make sure Manny is following us. Clay will meet us at the police station after he gets Sammy and Cleo settled at his farm. "I couldn't sleep and my phone was dead, so I drove to your house for company. I woke you up, you came downstairs, and we were sitting in your backyard talking when we saw Buster's pickup drive by."

"We'd better say we were on the front steps. You can't see the street from the back." It makes as much sense as anything else we've done this summer. "I got worried because of Ferret's unnatural interest in Miss Simmons—"

"Everything about Ferret is unnatural," Laurel points out.

"Too true. But in this case we decided to walk to her house and make sure she was okay. On the way we ran into Manny and Clay coming home from—"

"We won't think about that," Laurel cuts me off.

"From that point on, we'll tell what happened." She looks over at me and grins. "For once we don't even have to lie. We just leave out a few insignificant details."

If we keep our fingers and toes crossed, it might just work.

With Buster and Kong in jail—and Ferret on his way as soon as someone finds a store selling tomato juice in gallon jugs—Laurel and I don't hold anything back. Well, we skip over the pig incident since it's ancient history. And we use our new alibi story to explain the time we spent rescuing Cleo. But Laurel tells Officer Sierra the truth about the M-80s. I fill him in on the stalking, threats, and the pellets Buttferk shot into Carmine. After Clay arrives, all four of us tell our versions of what happened in Miss Simmons's house.

By the time we finish our official statements, dawn is breaking, and my heart rate has returned to normal. For the first time this summer, something actually went better than expected. Officer Sierra seemed to believe us about Buttferk, our parents didn't threaten capital punishment, and Clay promised to call me this afternoon.

Before we leave the police station, Officer Sierra asks to speak to me in private. As he leads me to his office, my pulse switches into overdrive. What does he know that I don't know he knows?

"I'm sure you're exhausted, Aspen. This will only take a minute." Officer Sierra's hair is matted, and his face is streaked with soot. He looks dead on his feet. "I'm sure it's no secret to you how Mr. Baumgarten came to be soaked with skunk spray."

"I . . . uh . . ."

"It's okay, Aspen. Everyone on the force knows about Miss Simmons's skunk. It's the worst-kept secret in town." He smiles, rearranging the creases of dirt around his mouth. "We just want to be sure the little guy is safe."

Is this a trick or—

"You don't have to look so suspicious. Honestly, I'm not trying to wring a confession out of you." Officer Sierra rolls his eyes in exasperation. "Tell you what—if Miss Simmons's *cat* is safe and in good hands, blink once. If not, blink twice."

I close my eyes once very deliberately.

"Thank you, Miss Parks. Now go home and get some sleep. I know I'm going to."

twenty-four

"DO YOU REALLY THINK MANNY WILL LIKE MY HAIR THIS color?" Laurel asks again as she twists herself into a corkscrew studying her reflection in my bedroom mirror. "Or will he think it's too ordinary?" Her short, razor-cut layers have been changed from strawberry red to her natural auburn, with a few subtle high- and lowlights scattered throughout.

Today is the first time we've seen each other since the fire at Miss Simmons's house six days ago. Miss Simmons spent the day and night after the fire in the hospital while the doctors ran some tests to make sure her concussion wasn't serious. She must not have been feeling too bad, because she called me three times to check on

Sammy. Each time she did, I had to phone Clay for an update, which was more than fine with me. When Miss Simmons was released from the hospital, she moved into the Cottonwood Inn, the town's only hotel, until her house is put back together. With repairmen swarming her place around the clock, I don't think the repairs will take long.

The morning after the fire Laurel's mom and step-dad picked her up on the way home from their Colorado camping trip and drove her to Chicago for a surprise visit before the beginning of school. We texted each other, but it was pretty inadequate considering everything we had to talk about. Now that she's back, there are more interesting topics to discuss than her hair color.

"For the millionth time, it looks great. But you're going to end up in traction if you keep contorting your neck like that." My hair has valiantly resisted Laurel's efforts with the curling wand and is doing its impersonation of whole-wheat spaghetti. But I can't help noticing my eyes. Thanks to this summer's adventures, their ordinary brown sparks with mischief and mystery.

"Come on, girls. It's time to go!" Mom calls from the bottom of the stairs. "You can't be late to your own ceremony."

My parents sit in the front seats of our SUV, Mr. Piedmont is in the second row, and Laurel and I take the back. While they babble about boring adult crap, Laurel and I exchange whispers.

Laurel slides over to me. "Clay says Cleo's doing okay, right?" Her breath is minty from my mouthwash.

"Cleo is having the time of her life." And so am I, with Clay calling every night to give me updates on Sammy and Cleo. "She and Rooster Cogburn, the resident chicken stud, have definitely found true love."

"Hmph!" Laurel sticks out her lower lip. "I guess it's okay, as long as Cleo doesn't forget about me." She leans in closer. "I sent EggstraGood a twenty-dollar bill from Chicago. That should give Steve's father something to wonder about."

"Good. We can close out that sordid chapter of our lives."

Dad pulls the car into the crowded police station parking lot, and my stomach gets queasy. The gray brick building looks pleasant enough, but I can't let go of the nagging fear that Officer Sierra is waiting by the door with two sets of shiny new handcuffs for Laurel and me.

Manny and Clay pull up in Clay's pickup as we're climbing out of the SUV. The plan was for them to change clothes at the golf course and meet us here. Clay smiles and waves at us. But instead of getting out when Manny does, Clay reaches over the seat, into the back of the cab.

As soon as Manny walks over, he flips on the charm switch with Laurel and her dad. He's blond and bronzed and, if he weren't my brother, I might be as giddy as Laurel seems. She hasn't heard—and smelled—Manny's farting demonstrations or experienced the delight of him scratching his crotch at breakfast. So why did Mr. Disgusting get all of the looks in the family?

Clay finishes whatever he was doing in the truck and joins us. I watch him work his way through the parent maze to end up beside me. His red-brown hair is damp, and freckles peek through his tan. "Hi, Aspen. It's great to see you." Clay's voice, low and intimate, makes my legs rubbery. Then our arms brush, and it's like touching a warm, tingly electric fence.

Feeling like an idiot, I manage a squeaky hello. I've never been happier that my parents can't tell what I'm thinking.

The police station lobby is packed with people and cameras. Mayor Danielson and several members of the city council stand in a cluster on one side of the lobby. Two police officers and several firefighters are lounging by the hallway that leads to the cells. Even Principal Hammond and some of the Cottonwood Creek High teachers are among the people in the crowd.

Laurel latches onto my arm. "Aspen, look!" she hisses

in my ear. "There are cameras from at least three TV stations here! We'll be all over tonight's news!"

Eyes turn toward the main entrance as Office Sierra walks in with Miss Simmons on his arm. Her hair is done up in old-lady curls, and she's wearing a flowered blue dress. A three-pronged cane has replaced the walker she's been using all summer. She stretches her neck, scanning the crowd, until she sees me.

I've talked to Miss Simmons on the phone at least twenty times since the fire, but the sight of her in one piece without her walker gives me a surprising rush of happiness. Even more amazing is that I'm honestly looking forward to having her as our neighbor again! Three months ago I couldn't have imagined being friends with that cranky old woman. Now I'm wiping away tears.

"Aspen Parks, there you are," she calls, dropping Officer Sierra's arm and waving. "Grab that boyfriend of yours and come over here. I want to talk to you both."

Everyone turns to look at me. My face is sizzling, and I'm rigid with embarrassment.

Clay places his palm on the middle of my back. "I think she means me," he whispers with a grin as wide as a watermelon wedge. "We should go talk to her before she announces our engagement." He reaches over and takes my hand.

"Okay." If my legs will stop trembling.

We trail after Miss Simmons and Officer Sierra as he escorts her to a padded chair on a raised platform at the far end of the room. As soon as she's seated, she dismisses him with typical Miss Simmons charm. "You've done your duty, Miguel. Now scoot over and talk to your police friends. I have something to discuss with these two young people."

Before Officer Sierra walks away, he catches my eye and . . . winks.

My mouth drops and hangs there until Miss Simmons grabs the sleeve of my only decent dress and nearly pulls me off my feet. "Is my Sammy eating and sleeping? I'm worried to death that he's pining away for me!"

Clay comes to my rescue. "Sammy's doing great, Miss Simmons. I set him up in a little pen in my backyard. I even put clean bedding in an old doghouse so he has a nice, comfortable place to sleep."

Miss Simmons clutches her chest and her face turns white. "You're making my poor Sammy live outdoors! He'll catch his death of cold!"

When it comes to mellowing out, she still has a way to go. "Skunks are supposed to live outside," I say in my most reasonable voice. "Besides, it's been ninety degrees all week."

Miss Simmons huffs and puffs before she finally says, "I suppose it will have to do until Monday. I'm told my house will be livable then, although I can't imagine how that crew of idiots will get rid of the smoke smell. Even so, anything will be better than putting up with another night in that vermin-infested Cottonwood Inn."

She pulls a blue handkerchief from her sleeve and wipes her forehead. "Thank goodness those three delinquents are going to get what's coming to them."

My ears prick up. "Oh? How's that?"

Miss Simmons wriggles her fingers for us to lean closer. "Miguel Sierra told me—in confidence—that the police believe those . . . those . . ."

"Buttferk," I offer helpfully. "That's what Laurel and I call them."

"Buttferk! How appropriate." Miss Simmons cackles. "Miguel says Buttferk is most likely responsible for burglaries in Redfield, Adel, and Winterset. It's going to be a cold day in Hades before they break into anyone else's house."

Mayor Danielson taps on a microphone set up next to where we're standing. "If I may have your attention, everyone, we'll begin the award ceremony."

Laurel and Manny wander over, and the four of us sit on the chairs beside Miss Simmons. After that, we're subjected to a round of speeches praising our bravery and courage, daring and valor, and every other synonym in *Roget's Thesaurus*.

My nose itches, my left butt cheek falls asleep, and there's more water under my armpits than in the Cottonwood Creek swimming pool. I sneak a side-glance at Clay, who may very well be praying for death. But Manny is beaming like a game show host, and Laurel is eating up the accolades like they're chocolate truffles.

After the speeches are finished, the police chief pins medals on the four "heroes," and we pose for enough pictures to clog the Internet for a week. TV reporters stick microphones and cameras in our faces and ask the same questions at least a dozen times. Manny and Laurel bask in the spotlight, mugging for the cameras and making witty comments. Clay looks ready to bolt for the nearest exit. I may beat him there.

When the hoopla finally ends, Miss Simmons drags Clay away, probably to give him more orders about Sammy's proper care and feeding. I'm about to follow when Laurel nudges me in the ribs. "Things between you and Clay seem to be going well."

"I suppose." Clay leans down to say something to Miss Simmons, and she actually laughs. "But, as friends or . . ." I don't want to jinx anything by saying it out loud.

"Yeah, he is kind of hard to read. Unlike your brother, whose intentions are perfectly clear." Laurel giggles. I tear my gaze away from Clay and look at her. Her face is flushed, her lipstick is smudged, and the hem of her blouse is sticking out. Until this second, I thought nothing was grosser than pig poop.

"Holy crap, Laurel, we're in the police station! Couldn't you guys wait ten more minutes?"

"Excuse me, girls," Officer Sierra says, and I jump about a foot. This guy has cornered the market on stealth. "May I talk to you for a minute?"

Laurel and I exchange glances and gulp in unison. We don't have much choice except to follow Officer Sierra into his office. After we're seated—on the edges of our chairs, with our eyes fixed on the door—he congratulates us again on saving Miss Simmons and rounding up Cottonwood Creek's equivalent of the James Gang.

"You know, ladies, there's been so much excitement, and official paperwork"—Officer Sierra blows out a sigh—"surrounding the incident at Miss Simmons's place that, until yesterday, I forgot about something unusual that happened the same night."

I will not make eye contact with Laurel. I will not make eye contact with Laurel. I will not . . .

"Oh, what was that?" Laurel's "that" comes out as a squeak.

"Funny you should ask, Laurel, because it involves the place where you used to work."

"The Sub Stop?" she asks, all innocence.

Good one, Laurel!

"Noooo." He drags it out until it sounds like three words. "The EggstraGood Chicken Farm. About thirty minutes before I got called to the B and E at Miriam Simmons's place, a call came in from a neighbor on a suspicious vehicle sighting at EggstraGood. It didn't sound particularly urgent, so I decided to finish my rounds before heading out there."

My arms are pressed tight against my sides to keep my sweat from dripping on the carpet. But if my heart stops and I keel over, he's going to know something's wrong.

"When all hell broke loose at Miriam's, I forgot all about it."

Laurel nods. "That's understandable." She's as cool as if they're discussing Cottonwood Creek's upcoming football season.

Officer Sierra cocks his head at her. "Then yesterday afternoon I got a call from Sid Turner, who owns EggstraGood. One of his workers found a roll of duct tape outside the electric fence. Sid wouldn't have thought a thing about it, except he got an envelope in the mail with a twenty-dollar bill inside. No message, just twenty bucks."

"Really?" Laurel isn't sounding quite so cool now.

"Really." He leans back and crosses one leg over the opposite knee. "Sid hasn't found any damage or anything missing, so, as far as I can see, there's no crime involved. I just thought it made an interesting story, especially since the manager told me you wanted to buy a chicken that was marked for slaughter."

Officer Sierra stands abruptly and straightens the creases in his pants. "Well, ladies, I'd better let you go. I'm sure you're anxious to go out and celebrate."

He opens the door for us. "Just so I have this straight— you're both going back to school tomorrow, right?"

Laurel and I both confirm that we are.

Officer Sierra looks up at the ceiling. "Thank God for small favors."

twenty-five

"WE'RE HERE, ASPEN! THE FIRST DAY OF OUR LAST YEAR OF high school." Laurel straightens the mirror she hung in our locker and checks her reflection.

Sam and Tyler step out of the hallway throng and stop near us. They're wearing the senior fall uniform of baggy khaki shorts and wrinkled polos. And, while they don't look much better than they did at the barn kegger, they appear to be reasonably sober.

"Hello there, lovely ladies," Sam drawls. "You looked mighty fine on the tube last night, Aspen." He looks me up and down with his eyes half-closed. He's either trying to look sexy or is suffering from pink eye. "Mighty fine."

"As did you, Laurel. And you look even finer this

morning." Tyler attempts a leer while he scratches the five hairs growing on his upper lip.

It wouldn't be cool to start off my senior year by making a rude remark. "Uh, thanks . . . I guess."

"You are more than welcome." Sam bows from the waist, climbing two more rungs up the dork ladder.

"Later." Tyler tips an imaginary hat as they resume their hallway strut.

When they're out of earshot, Laurel rolls her eyes and says, "Can't be late enough for me." She slams our locker shut. "I told you if we did something to get noticed during the summer it would lead to an outstanding senior year," Laurel adds as she tugs her shorts over her butt cheeks. "And everything worked out exactly the way I planned it."

My mind travels back to yesterday. After our families went out to lunch together, Clay offered to drive me home, and I raced to his pickup before my parents could veto the idea. When he asked if I wanted to take a detour to his farm to see Sammy and Cleo, I was so excited I almost lost my lunch. But I maintained my usual cool exterior and only stammered a little.

He showed me his prairie plantings, the resident farm cats, and his recent animal arrivals. Sammy, curled up inside his doghouse, barely opened his eyes when I scratched his head. And Cleo—whose wing tag had been discreetly removed—was much more interested in Rooster Cogburn than in either of us.

After we said our hellos to the animals, Clay and I walked down to the wooden bridge overlooking Cottonwood Creek. The leaves in Clay's patch of woods flashed green and silver tinged with the first hints of autumn red. Silvery minnows swam through the shallow water, and a painted turtle watched us from a rotting log before slipping into the creek. It was peaceful and shady, with the soothing sound of moving water. And when Clay held me close and kissed me, it became my favorite place on Earth.

Next weekend is his family's annual Labor Day picnic at the farm. My parents are invited, along with Laurel, her dad, and Miss Simmons. Manny will be there, too. He's coming home to visit after only one week at Iowa State. But Laurel may have something to do with that.

Laurel's selective memory is working as well as ever. There's no way she could plan a summer as bizarre as ours. "Let's just say I won't complain about the way it ended."

As we make our way to our first classes, Miss Noonbottom sweeps toward us. Her flowered dress seems tighter and shorter than it did last spring. Knowing too well how often she drops her baton, I fear for this year's vocal music students.

Miss Noonbottom stops in the middle of the hall, blocking traffic in both directions. "Well, if it isn't

Cottonwood Creek's newest celebrities." She beams at us. "You girls made quite a splash on last evening's news. Quite a splash."

"Thank you, Miss Noonbottom," Laurel and I say together.

She lowers her voice. "I heard a rumor—from a very reliable source—that Principal Hammond is going to call an assembly in your honor this afternoon."

"That's awesome!" Laurel fluffs up her hair. "Thanks for telling us."

"Don't mention it." Miss Noonbottom looks around and notices the traffic jam behind her. "Well, I must be off to class. I'll see you young heroes later today."

"Listen to that," Laurel says as we step aside to let her walk past. "She even remembers us."

Miss Noonbottom stops and wags her finger. "Now, Aster and Lily, you mustn't dally. I expect you girls to set a good example for your classmates."

Laurel sputters, but Miss Noonbottom is intent on getting to the music room.

"I see what you mean, Laurel," I say, suppressing a chuckle. "Now that we're famous, our senior year is going to be completely different."

acknowledgments

I AM BLESSED TO HAVE THE SUPPORT AND AFFECTION
of a number of resilient, insightful women—and men—
who lift me up in so many ways. Thank you for honoring
me with your friendship.

My everlasting love and gratitude go to my magical
writing group: Sharelle Byars Moranville, Eileen Boggess,
and Rebecca Janni. You are talented authors, amazing
women, and priceless friends.

I have the deepest admiration and respect for my
incredible agent, Rosemary Stimola, for your humor,
knowledge of all things publishing, and your belief in me.
I still pinch myself to see if I'm dreaming.

Thank you to my brilliant editor, Ruth Katcher, whose
insight, kindness, and patience made revising easy. Working with you is a delight.

Thanks also to the outstanding team at Egmont USA: managing editor Nico Medina, assistant editor Alison Weiss, and copyeditor Sandra Smith. For city folks, you do a real good job.

Special thanks to Chief Larry Phillips of the Waukee Police Department for patiently answering my questions about juvenile offenders. Please excuse the liberties I took with police procedures.

A bonus thank-you to my brother Dan who—brave soul that he is—reads every manuscript I send him.

And a big hug and kiss to my forever guy, Mike. I know you'll see this eventually.